MURDER IN INYO COUNTY

MURDER IN INYO COUNTY

(JIM COBB MYSTERY #1)

by

Mike Nails

The Conrad Press

Murder In Inyo County
Published by The Conrad Press in the United Kingdom 2023
Tel: +44(0)1227 472 874
www.theconradpress.com info@theconradpress.com
ISBN 978-1-916966-08-6
Copyright ©Blackthorne Crossing LLC 2023 All rights reserved.
Typesetting and Cover Design by: Levellers

The Conrad Press logo was designed by Maria Priestley.
Printed and bound in Great Britain by Clays Ltd, Elcograf S.p.A.

*To my three children, Thomas, Laura, and Amanda,
who are always there by my side with your laughter, insight,
and integrity. I can't do it without each of you.*

Sherlock Holmes: 'How often have I said to you that when you
have eliminated the impossible, whatever remains, however
improbable, must be the truth?'

—Sir Arthur Conan Doyle

MURDER IN INYO COUNTY

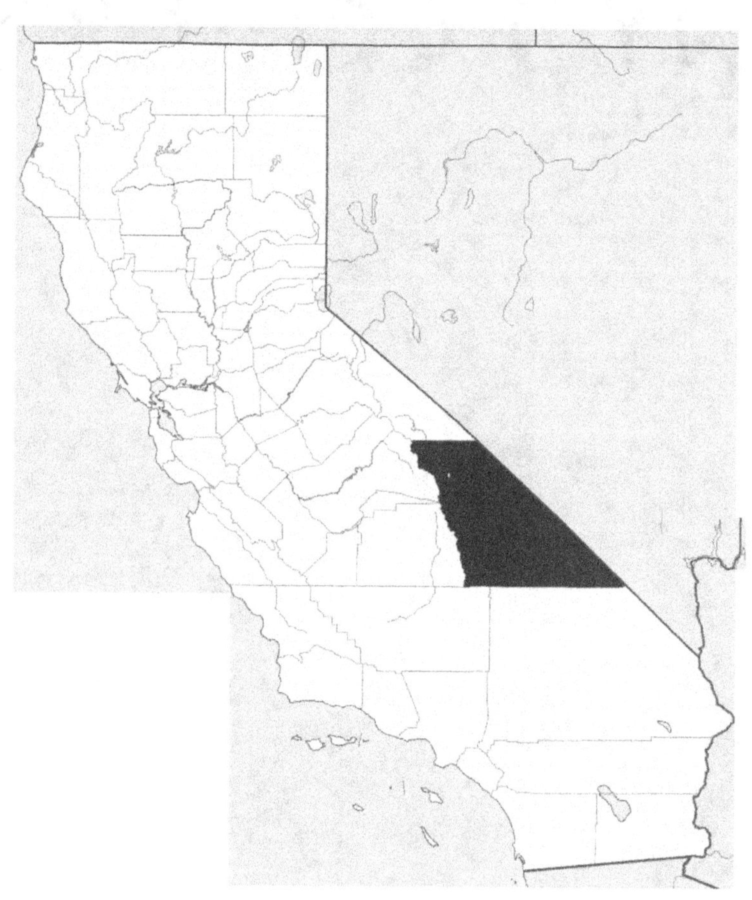

CHAPTER 1

The eastern High Sierra Mountains of California were silent in the last half of October 1957. Inyo County turned colder at night now, causing an early dusting of snow on the highest mountain peaks.

The Inyo County Sheriff's Department in the high desert had been deathly quiet over the previous thirty-six hours. Before six a.m., Tuesday, October 22nd, a call came in. Marlene Chambers, the dispatch operator, answered with the usual greeting.

'Hello, Inyo County Sheriff's Office.'

The voice on the other end of the line was male. 'Send someone out to the old Conroy Ranch off Pine Creek Road, ten miles west of Bishop. A robbery took place there. The owner is waiting in the barn.'

'What's your name, sir?' The caller hung up.

Marlene clicked the phone to get the switchboard operator. 'Where did the last call come from?'

'In Bishop. A pay phone at the gas station. That's all I know.'

'Thanks.' Marlene hung up and dialed Jasper 'Red' Fowler, the county's acting sheriff.

'Red, I just received an anonymous call from a man up in Bishop.'

'What about?'

'They reported a robbery at the old Conroy Ranch off Pine Creek Road.'

Marlene knew less than three hundred people lived in the area west of Bishop. The sheriff's office has a patrol division substation there, a little over forty miles north of the main sheriff's office in Independence.

'Do we have a cruiser out in the area?'

'We do, Red. It's that young fellow, Perry Rimmer.' 'Call and tell him to take a look at the situation.'

Rimmer drove toward the towering High Sierra Mountains to the west and felt the chill of an early winter coming. The cold morning wind was blowing a few tumbleweeds over the arid land, as though no one had lived there for several years. He found the ranch house deserted, rundown, animals gone.

He made his way to the barn, pulling up the collar on his jacket, and put his palm on the handle of his standard issue .38 Smith & Wesson revolver.

The rolling hinges protested as Rimmer used his back to push open the door far enough to enter. He walked through the dusty, deserted entrance, past an empty tack room loaded with cobwebs, and stood in the open aisle in front of several abandoned horse stalls, three on each side. Silence prevailed, except for the wind blowing against the dilapidated, creaking wooden structure.

The barn was dirty, with old stalks of hay mixed in with long dried-out horse manure. Rimmer moved toward the back of the stable and looked up to see that part of the roof had been blown away, leaving a large hole, which allowed the early morning light to reach the floor.

At the back end of the barn, the walkway formed the top of a T-shaped aisle. Rimmer turned to his left and discovered the reason for the call to the Sheriff's Office. A man was hanging upside down, his feet tied together, his hands tied behind his back. The body was cold, but not stiff. The head hung roughly a foot off the barn floor, and a large pool of blackened dried blood congealed in the dirt directly below it.

Rimmer saw a large slash across the neck from ear to ear— it showed rivulets of dried blood. He moved over to an empty area of the walkway, away from the body, before he threw up his breakfast.

CHAPTER 2

That morning, when Rimmer drove out to the old Conroy Ranch, Merrill Cobb was eating his favorite breakfast of huevos rancheros. His son Jim, sitting opposite him, was sipping coffee, his breakfast untouched. Jim was thirty-seven, six feet tall, with dark brown hair that frequently fell across his green eyes. He was muscular, but not overtly so.

Merrill, at six foot seven and two hundred-fifty pounds, one of the biggest men in Inyo County, was first elected sheriff in 1920 and retired in 1956. Merrill had hazel eyes and a full head of white hair, chiseled facial features, and a solid muscular body. He was sitting at his customary seat at the head of the table, holding up his empty cup. 'I'll have some more, Conchita.'

Conchita Ramirez, thirty, had been the ranch's housekeeper and cook for thirteen years. She filled Merrill's cup with the hot liquid. Her eyes looked away; her face blank.

She wasn't talking, and definitely not getting close to Merrill.

Merrill put down his cup as the phone rang in the den. 'You got this, son?'

Jim shook his head.

Merrill let out a grunt of displeasure as he rose to answer it. 'I've got a call from the acting sheriff,' said the switchboard operator at the other end.

'I'll take it,' Merrill said, 'put him on.'

He paused, listening to the caller. 'We'll be ready. Ten minutes.'

Merrill returned to the kitchen and sat down. His face showing nothing, he finished his coffee.

'Red Fowler called,' he said finally. 'There was a murder up near Bishop. He'll be here in ten minutes. We need to go.'

Red Fowler was Jim Cobb's assistant chief and oldest deputy, having worked for years alongside Jim's Dad, Merrill.

Red was a big, burly, grizzled man with worn, dried out skin from years in the low humidity sunshine of the high desert. He had thick wrinkles around his eyes, and a high balding forehead with the rest of his existing hair around his ears. His hair had turned from his namesake red to white after the news of the Pearl Harbor sneak attack hit the airwaves.

Red never married and had given his life to working as a deputy sheriff. After Harriet and Kendall had died, he was the most likely choice for interim sheriff—he knew more about the department than any other deputy.

Now, at the age of sixty-three, Red was interim chief and not happy about it. He had no political aspirations, he wanted to work for Jim Cobb. Now, if he could only get Jim Cobb back in the office, off the liquor, and make him take back the job as sheriff of Inyo County.

The late morning sun shone through the narrow spaces between the dried-out, unpainted wooden walls of the barn, now filled with Sheriff's Department personnel. Acting Sheriff Red Fowler, retired Sheriff Merrill Cobb, and his son, the forlorn looking Jim, were silent.

The California Department of Justice Laboratory (Criminal Identification & Information Unit) in Sacramento arrived mid-afternoon to offer expertise on fingerprints and forensics.

The funeral director from Lone Pine, a Mr. Earl Adams, was the last to arrive.

Inyo County didn't have its own medical examiner. Instead, Los Angeles County sent up theirs when necessary. The makeshift office was in the basement at the Lone Pine Funeral Home. This arrangement had served the county since 1920, the same year Merrill had been elected sheriff for the first time.

At the old Conroy Ranch the weather was turning colder, and signs of rigor mortis had nearly dispersed. They knew that death had occurred three days earlier.

'Shit, it's starting again,' Merrill told Red. 'Sure looks like it,' Red replied.

'I should have solved it. Five murders in ten years, no clues, no suspects. The fucker comes back now, after fifteen years?' Merrill looked at Red, frowning. 'Where was he all this time?'

Red shrugged. 'Maybe in jail for something else. Or he moved to a different part of the country. This could be a different killer altogether. An apprentice? Or a copycat?'

'If you're right, Red, Inyo County is in for a world of hurt.' 'Whatever it is, it's Jim's case now,' Red replied.

Merrill gazed at his son, shook his head and looked back at Red. 'It will be Jim's case if he gets his head out of his ass and returns to work.'

'He will, Merrill. He'll do it,' Red said, hoping for the same thing.

CHAPTER 3

As the sheriff of Inyo County, I was compelled to make my presence known.

Sitting on an upturned crate at the edge of the crime scene, I hadn't had a drop of liquor to drink yet and was starting to feel a little shaky. My bereavement leave was to last another two weeks, and I didn't want any involvement with this investigation.

I made my last visit to the Lone Pine Liquor Store five days before, when I picked up four bottles of Bourbon. I'd done the same every three to four days since the death of my wife and child.

While walking out, I'd bumped into a stranger coming through the door in the opposite direction, knocking him to the floor.

Around forty, gaunt in appearance, he wore a three-day-old beard, and a sweat-rimmed cowboy hat that fell off his head. A jagged scar ran from the outer edge of his left eye diagonally to the side of his nose. The old repair was haphazard, and poorly done, leaving thickened overlapped tissue where the uneven edges didn't match up. His old work clothes and boots fitted his demeanor perfectly.

I helped the hopeless looking outsider to his feet. 'You okay?'

The man held out his hand. 'Yeah, I'm okay. Can you spare some change for an out of work veteran?'

'Sure.' I fished a few dollars bills out of my pocket and gave him the money.

We went off in opposite directions. I didn't think much of our chance meeting.

The dead man hanging from the barn's rafters in front of me had the same jagged scar under his left eye. I knew instantaneously. The victim was the man I'd bumped into in front of the Lone Pine Liquor Store five days earlier.

CHAPTER 4

The investigation wore on to the early evening. Department of Justice State Crime Scene personnel from Sacramento examined the barn and the surrounding area. The technicians of the fledgling science spent the rest of that day and the next working on the scant amount of evidence they found.

There were no fingerprints, no tire tracks, and no material left at the scene to indicate any specific individual or individuals. The rope used could have been bought at any hardware or feed store in the state.

The Inyo Sheriff's Department was placed, again, in a waiting game, without leads, suspects, or information about the identity of the killer.

The body was taken to the funeral home in Lone Pine and put in a cooler to wait for the traveling medical examiner to come up from Los Angeles County.

The FBI was called in to assist the Inyo County Sheriff's Office. The Bureau wanted to keep a tight lid on the news of the murder. Theo Culpepper, who worked in the San Bernardino's Sheriff Office until 1939, when he joined the FBI after completing law school, was the assigned special agent for the Hanging Murders.

Theo was Red's cousin, and they grew up together on Red's family ranch in Shoshone, a small town with only a handful of people, southeast of Death Valley. The two men were like brothers and the camaraderie they shared was palpable.

Theo stood at six-two, one hundred eighty-five pounds, with a raw-boned body, like a thoroughbred racehorse. His face was all sharp angles, thin mouth, a long nose with straight edges, and amber colored eyes. The man stood out in a crowd, purposeful, direct, and assertive.

Red and Theo exchanged pleasantries and the details of the case, back to the beginning.

The first Hanging Murder had occurred in 1932. Now, fifteen years after the last one, this case marked a new Hanging Murder in Inyo County.

Red was trying to make sense of everything. So many questions ran through his head he couldn't think straight. Then a new question pushed all others aside. Was this also connected to the robberies of the Hollywood people when they came here up to shoot one of their big movies?

The murders went on for ten years, stopped, and now started again. The robberies never stopped, were never solved, and there were no apprehensions of any suspects. Barton Haskel had been the lead investigator on the robberies, until his retirement in 1950.

The robberies had slowed down over the last seven years, from eight or nine a year to only three last year, and one this year. Could the Hanging Murderer and the robberies be connected? Was the same guy doing both? Or was there an accomplice or accomplices?

Red shook his head to clear it. This was too much for him. He needed to talk with Jim and Merrill; and possibly even

Barton, to flesh out his ideas and come to some logical conclusion. Put to rest his wild ideas or find the murderer and the robbery ring.

Red Fowler knew that he and the sheriff's department were sinking into quicksand. The good people of Inyo County needed Sheriff Jim Cobb back on the job.

Red Fowler needed Jim back on the job, too.

A killer had to be found, and this was too much for Red to handle.

CHAPTER 5

The drive north on California Route 395 was beautiful in the early morning, just that beginning light between night and sunrise. The sun would peek over the edge of Mono Lake, the large, shallow saline body of water bordering the California and Nevada line.

On the lake's southwest shore lay the little community of Lee Vining, home to no more than one-hundred and sixty souls. The only coffee shop in town was The Lakes, open at five a.m., every day of the year. Large plate glass windows facing toward where Mono Lake was located would release the warmth of the rising sun into the shop.

On this particular morning, the air was cooler than normal. A 1940 Chevy pickup truck, its dark blue color now almost gone from wind and sun erosion, stopped in front of the small shop for breakfast.

The driver appeared older than his years, wore a three-day growth of stubble, dusty work clothes, and well-worn cowboy boots. As he entered the restaurant, he took off his weathered Stetson hat, revealing his close-cropped salt 'n pepper hair.

The restaurant only had a few customers. Taking an unoccupied booth toward the back, he ordered the homemade corned beef hash, two eggs over easy on top, country potatoes, buttered white toast with homemade jam, and plenty of strong black coffee. He stayed a little over an hour and a half.

'Anything else, hon?' asked the waitress.

'No, I'll just have one more cup and the check, ma'am.'

The man rolled a cigarette with his own fixings and lit the end with a wooden match from a little cardboard box. He sucked in a deep breath, held the hot corrosive discharge for a while before letting the smoke out into the air above his head in several perfect '0' rings, as he stared at the waitress as he contemplated what he wanted to accomplish next.

No one rushed the man from his booth as he drank the last of the strong coffee. Satisfied with the meal and his smoke, he rose from the booth, leaving enough money for the bill and a tip. He seated his hat on his head and went out the door.

Still smiling to himself, he opened the door of his truck, and started the ancient Chevy's straight-six engine.

Outside the little ranching town of Bridgeport, a young woman was hitchhiking home.

He stopped the truck and offered her a ride.

Before settling in the seat, the endless chatter started. The young woman's nonstop discourse told of hopes, dreams, and what was going to happen in her life.

After a few minutes, he tired of her prattle. Pulling over to the side of the road, and physically overwhelming her, he silenced the incessant blather. Without a sound, he killed her with a pocketknife.

He drove the Chevy farther north, past Lake Topaz, which sat astride the border of Nevada and California. Turning right on Nevada State Route 208, he drove east to Wellington for dinner and a night's stay at a small inn.

# # #

The body of the young woman was found four days later in a drainage ditch a mere ten yards off the highway. Her entrails were pulled out from her abdomen. Her eyes were wide open; the cooler weather had caused a glassy film to cover them.

The local authorities found no identification with the body or any fingerprints, nor was she physically abused.

The body was identified after her photo appeared in the area newspapers. Her name was Rachel Parker, fifteen years old, a high school sophomore. She was from the outlying area ranch.

Rachel Parker's family had placed her name in the missing person file at the Bridgeport police station twenty-four hours after she had failed to return home. She had been missing for five days before her family saw the picture in the weekly paper.

Time passed, but the family never found closure for their daughter's murder.

CHAPTER 6

The Cowboy Bar & Grill was a long-established watering hole in Lone Pine, dating back to the repeal of Prohibition in 1933. Originally it was a little oasis, a getaway from the day-to-day life in the high desert.

It was a good-sized establishment, with a long mahogany bar and dark wooden stools, a shadowy sitting area with eight booths around the back wall, and ten tables with four chairs each. In January 1940, the bar had expanded into the unused space next door, allowing for a full kitchen tucked out of the way behind the bar area, and a place to play pool. The decor was Western. Real branding irons hung from the walls, along with saddles, ropes, chaps, and hats mixed in, to make an authentic statement.

No one in town knew that a movie set designer had created all the atmosphere the owner wanted. Lone Pine was the community where westerns and adventure movies came to fruition. Paying homage to the lifestyle played into the minds of the locals. Any Hollywood types who came to town for a film shoot lost themselves in the local establishment. The Cowboy Bar & Grill was a place for both groups—locals and out-of-towners.

Grady Bennett, the Hollywood Beat reporter for the Los Angeles Post was sitting at the bar in the Cowboy Bar & Grill. It was seven p.m. on Friday night, October 25th.

Ever since Grady had arrived in the high desert area of Lone Pine, he'd seen reminders of the Old West. The movies that were made out at Movie Flats. The western dress of all the locals. Even the Cowboy Bar & Grill had Old West paraphernalia on the walls. Ranches, horses, and sweat from hard working men who worked out on the range—the stuff of movies—were real here.

Grady was tall and slim and wore his blond hair long, over his ears, and his sapphire blue eyes made women seek him out. At least that was his experience in Los Angeles. The thirty-five-year-old single news-man was looking around the room for the prospect of finding someone to warm his bed later.

Grady was on assignment for the paper, and his task was to talk with the locals about a new Randolph Scott western called *Ride Lonesome*, due for release in February. The crew had filmed all the outside scenes in and around Lone Pine for six weeks the previous spring. Grady's job was to find out any gossip from the locals about the film, its stars, or the production company, that would make a good story for the newspaper.

Grady was tired of being a catch-em-in-the-act Hollywood gos-sip reporter. Someone who followed the salacious goings-on of the famous and near famous of Hollywood. Grady wanted to be a byline news reporter.

Nursing a tumbler of cheap rye neat, he called the barkeeper over for a chat. 'Howdy, partner, I'm doing a feature article on the latest Randolph Scott picture. Care to talk about the film?'

'I'm Barton Haskel, part owner and chief barkeep of this here estab-lishment. There is no news about that movie or any other.'

'Hold on, mister,' Grady said, holding up his hands. 'I didn't mean to upset the neighborhood. I'm just an honest guy, trying to do my job.'

Barton snorted. 'We here in Lone Pine don't want to talk about anything involving the movie industry. Hollywood came to this town about 1920 and filmed *The Roundup*, a silent picture starring Fatty Arbuckle and Wallace Berry. Since then, over two-hundred films have been made here.'

'That's a great history lesson, Mister Barkeep, but what is the real scoop on the Randolph Scott movie?'

'There is no scoop. Finish your drink and get out of my bar, understand?'

'Sure, sure, Mr. Haskel. I understand.' Grady slowly sipped his drink as an attractive woman in her early thirties came in and sat a couple of seats down from him.

The woman called out. 'Hey, Barton, give me a Canadian whiskey Manhattan. I've got news for you.'

Her loud voice caught Grady's ear, and his head perked up.

Barton made the Manhattan cocktail and placed it in front of the woman. 'Here, Edith. What news do you have that I can't get from the radio?'

'The Hanging Murderer has returned.' 'What the hell are you talking about?'

Edith Pearson, in her early thirties, had been secretary to the Inyo County sheriff for nine years. She dressed well on her salary and she always had a new car. She was feisty, in your face, fun to be around, but if she was saying something, it was true.

'Red Fowler told me all about it. The sheriff's office found another Hanging Murder victim out at the old Conroy Ranch out by Bishop three days ago. The state boys and the FBI want it kept under wraps. Red had to agree with the news blackout since Jim is still on leave.'

'Did Red say if it was like the others?' Barton asked.

Grady had never heard of any Hanging Murders. How many? Where? When? What were the details? Maybe this was his big chance to get out of the Hollywood Beat section and onto the front page. He moved one stool closer to the woman and waited for more.

'Red said this one was just like all the others. Red and Merrill are frantic about the return of the murderer.' She looked up at Barton. 'They also want Jim to get back to work. You're his best friend, tell him to get his ass back to work.'

'Jim's fine. He just needs a little time to recover.'

'Hell, Barton, it's been four months since Harriet and Kendall died.'

'Give the man a break, Edith; he lost his wife and kid.'

'You know I love Jim Cobb as much as you. He's my boss. The man is a helluva lot better sheriff than his father ever was.' Edith paused, 'I always had to keep Merrill's hands off me in the office. He wasn't like you were. I still get all warm and fuzzy when I think about you and me together.'

Barton smiled. 'Yeah, we had a good run, but that was then, and we've both moved on.'

A customer at the other end of the bar called out. 'Hey, Barton, you working or jawing? We need another round down here.'

'Keep your shirt on, Rowdy, I'm on my way.' Turning to Edith, he said, 'Now I have to go make a living.' He put his hand on her cheek, she held his hand as she turned her head into his palm and kissed it.

Grady watched the display of intimacy, thinking this was one woman he wouldn't mind sharing his bed with.

Barton went to the other end of the bar as Edith took another sip of her cocktail.

'Pardon my impudence, ma'am, but I couldn't help overhearing your conversation.' Now Grady was looking into Edith's green eyes. 'My name is Grady Bennett, and I'm a reporter for the Post in LA.'

'I'm Edith Pearson, Sheriff Jim Cobb's secretary. Glad to meet you.' They shook hands and laughed at their introductions. Edith looked at the new man in town with interest, feeling a sudden warmth run through her body.

'Can I buy you a drink?' Grady asked.

'Yes, you can, Mister Newspaperman Grady Bennett.' 'Let's find a quiet booth and get to know each other better, Miss Edith Pearson.'

Barton watched Edith and Grady pick up their drinks and find a secluded booth as far away from the bar as possible. The retired deputy sheriff was glad his onetime lover and the newspaper reporter moved to the back of the barroom. Tonight, the last thing Barton needed was for Edith to get any hairbrained ideas. When he saw Edith's foot kick out of a shiny new high heel and he knew she would rub a nylon stockinged foot up and down the reporter's leg, he knew he didn't have to worry about the possibility of an after-closing rendezvous.

She and Barton had begun meeting shortly after she'd started working at the sheriff's office. The affair between the two singles had lasted two years, ending mutually and without any animosity. But now and then, the two would get together for old times' sake and have a few wild days in a hideaway.

Barton knew that Edith was a woman who wanted to live life without any restrictions. A man was only as good as the fun she had with him. Marriage and children were not in her grand plan for happiness. One day at a time for the willowy, five-foot-seven woman with the jade green eyes and brunette hair. Same for the slim blond Los Angeles reporter.

Barton, in contrast, was broad in the shoulders, muscular, and tall at six feet. Like Grady and Edith, he had never married, had no kids, and didn't want any. His brown eyes and weathered face made him look strong. Nearly fifty, he was free and wild. There were many local women, until one truly captured his heart. She was Lara Aartz, from San Diego, daughter of a retired diplomat who hated Barton's guts.

Barton and Lara met years earlier, when Barton was working an extracurricular security job for a Majestic Pictures World Premiere event in Lone Pine in 1949 and Lara was there as eye candy. They had met surreptitiously every other weekend or so in San Diego.

Grady pumped Edith with questions about Lone Pine. She answered them all. Several rounds of Manhattans and straight rye whiskeys were sent back to the table. After a time, Grady had gathered a fair amount of information about the Hanging Murders.

Jim Cobb came in right after Edith and Grady had found their secluded booth. The sheriff ordered his usual, Four Roses. After about an hour, Jim finished his fourth round, not talking, just staring at nothing. Just after midnight, Barton wiped the top of the bar with a cloth and told Jim, 'I think it's time for you to mosey on back home, pardner.'

Jim picked his head up and looked at Barton. 'You're a good friend.'

Juan Pérez, the ever-present cook, came from the kitchen. 'Take the Sheriff home, Juan. Use his truck and go home. You can drive it back here in the morning, you're opening up. He can pick it up tomorrow.'

'Si, Señor Barton.'

Barton helped Jim out of the bar and into his truck for the drive home. He was back inside, rubbing down the bar, when Darren Harris, the bar's new co-owner, came out from the office behind the kitchen. Darren, a successful movie producer at Majestic Pictures, was going to be in town just until the next morning, before heading back to Los Angeles. 'Who's the lush you and Juan helped out of here?'

'That's the sheriff,' Barton replied. 'Does he get drunk like that often?'

Barton nodded. 'Almost every day for the last four months.

Since he lost his family.'

Darren watched the truck's taillights disappear. 'What happened?'

'His wife and daughter were killed driving to Los Angeles.' Barton glanced at Darren. 'She was leaving him for a history professor at UCLA, of all things.'

'That's an interesting story. Sounds like a movie plot.'

Barton replied, 'She wanted more than a cowboy sheriff in the wild high country, I guess.'

He noticed two young ranch hands, Oakley and Mason, were having a heated discussion about the woman who was drinking with them. When the men began throwing punches, Barton was able to force them out of the bar and into the parking lot out front.

'Get out of town and back to your bunkhouse. And stay the hell out of my bar!'

Oakley yelled out, 'I'll come back and take care of you, Haskel! This ain't the last of it!'

Barton waved his hand in disgust, turning his back on them, and went back inside, laughing to himself about the cheap threat made by a drunken ranch hand. People inside the bar, and the other workers, had all seen the ruckus and heard the threat. Including Darren Harris.

A few hours later, Barton said, 'Last call. Anyone want a final drink?'

Edith and Grady heard the request as they stumbled out of the bar, holding each other up. Grady's mind was no longer on the Hanging Murderer. They made their way across the street to Grady's room at the Mount Whitney Motel. Grady had a tough time finding the keyhole. After a couple of tries, he was able to unlock the door, turn on the light, and help Edith inside.

She took off her shoes and sat on the bed, rubbing her feet on the chenille bedspread as he put on the light in the bathroom and left the door ajar. The mood was set.

Edith was propped up on a couple of pillows, holding a cigarette. 'Come on over here and give a girl a light.'

CHAPTER 7

On the same day the Task Force started working on the Hanging Murders, Grady woke up and saw the sleeping Edith in his bed. He smiled at the thought of the previous night. She looked serene and innocent, her pouty lips and little upturned nose resting just above the edge of the sheet. Grady watched Edith's rhythmic breathing, every muscle in his body hurting from the night before. Edith was the freest spirit, and most anything goes woman Grady had ever met.

Grady was sitting up on the bed with the sheet covering his lower half. When Edith rolled over in her sleep, he kissed her on her shoulder, starting to work his way up her neck.

Edith murmured, 'I hope the man from Los Angeles wants more than just a little wake-up smooch.'

'What, by chance, did you have in mind?' he asked, smiling at her.

After they showered and dressed, they went back across the street to the Cowboy Bar & Grill. Saturdays and Sundays were the days when the Grill served its special brunch. The spread was an all-you-can-eat buffet with a country theme: waffles, pancakes, French toast, eggs any way you wanted them, every meat available from steak to hash, sausage to ham, thick homemade bread for toasting, and strong coffee. Juan Pérez, the Cowboy Bar & Grill's cook, made everything from scratch with the help of his wife and kids.

Edith and Grady sat at the same booth they had enjoyed the night before as they ate their breakfast. Juan's youngest daughter went around to each table and refilled the customers' outstretched cups.

Edith called out, 'Maria, we'll take some more coffee, please. ¿Dónde está su padre?'

'He is in the back cooking, Señorita Edith.' 'Ask your father to come by our table.'

'Sí, Señorita Edith, I will tell him.' Maria replied, as she left.

'It sounds like you have breakfast here often,' Grady said. 'Lone Pine is a small community, and the locals support all

the businesses. And of course, Juan makes the best breakfast in town.'

Edith smiled, showing off her small dimples above the edge of her upper lip. She didn't want to say anything to upset what she hoped would be the beginning of a beautiful relationship with the newspaper reporter.

Juan came out from the kitchen and came briskly over to their booth. '¡Hola! Señorita Edith. How you are?'

'Very well, thank you. This is a great breakfast.' She pointed across the table. 'This is my friend, Grady Bennett.'

'Muchas gracias, Señorita Edith, Buenos dias, Señor Bennett.'

Grady smiled at the cook.

Edith smiled. '¿Dónde está Señor Barton?'

'He no come to work today. I open today. I come back to the restaurant with Señor Jim's truck this morning.'

'Gracias, Juan.'

'De nada.' Juan hurried back to the kitchen.

'Huh, that's strange,' Edith told Grady, as she sipped her java. 'Barton is always here, having breakfast Saturday mornings.'

'Maybe he slept in,' Grady offered.

'That's always a possibility,' she replied.

Grady rubbed his stomach. 'More than enough for me.

Ready to go?'

'Let me take you for a tour of the movie location sites. We can gather your things at the motel and bring them to my place. I want to change my clothes.'

That was fine with Grady. He decided to keep the per diem money the newspaper would spend on a motel for him.

They left the Cowboy Bar & Grill, only needing to walk to the other side of the street to collect Grady's belongings. The couple rode in Edith's 1953 baby blue Chevrolet Bel Air convertible. The car had a three-speed automatic transmission, power steering, and a new one-piece windshield. They drove straight to Edith's little bungalow on the eastern side of Lone Pine.

After leaving his Royal Quiet De Luxe portable typewriter in the living room, Grady placed his worn suitcase in the bedroom and looked toward Edith across the bed.

'As much as I enjoyed our little tête-à-tête before breakfast,' she said 'I think we both need to take a spin around town and the surrounding area before we settle in.

'Okay. What should we see?' asked Grady.

'Inyo County has been a location site for almost forty years. Movies have been shot here, from Bishop to Death Valley, Manzanar to Mount Whitney, but the most used area has been the Alabama Hills Location and in particular the Movie Flats just west of Lone Pine.'

Grady laughed, 'Show me the way, Miss Tour Guide.'

They drove west from the center of town on Lone Pine Creek Road. Edith told him they were looking at the snow-capped peaks of the high Sierras, where Mount Whitney was the highest peak in the United States.

'The Alabama Hills area covers the next twelve miles north,' Edith explained to him. 'The odd-shaped boulders and stone pinnacles portray everything from the old west desert settings to a far-flung vision of the Far East.' Driving onward, she continued, 'The Movie Flats area includes the locations for the filming of *Lives of the Bengal Lancer and Gunga Din. Further on, High Sierra, Charge of the Light Brigade, and The Lone Ranger* were filmed.'

Edith wanted to show Grady one last famous area in the Flats, Randolph Scott's Rock. She stopped her car, went around to the back, and removed a large woolen blanket from the trunk. 'I'll put this down over here in the shade. We can pretend we are two lovers hiding from the bad guys.'

The afternoon outdoors had tired them both. They arrived back at Edith's house, relaxed in a leisurely bath, and slept before finding a place for dinner.

CHAPTER 8

I was thinking about this past 4th of July. On that date, my wife of twelve years, Harriet, and our daughter Kendall, who's twelfth birthday was just six weeks earlier, both died. The two women in my life were taken away in a horrific car crash. Harriet had been driving with Kendall to Los Angeles.

Harriet had left me a handwritten note on the dresser beside the bed. We lived in a two-bedroom bungalow, in Owens Valley, south of Lone Pine, California.

Our home was three-hundred yards from my parents' house, the main house on the ranch, completed before I returned from England in '46, from the war, with Harriet and the baby. In total, my parents had roughly five-thousand acres, and five-hundred head pure bred Black Angus cattle, as well as a couple of prize bulls.

For the U.S., the war had commenced after Pearl Harbor and like all the young men in America, I wanted to join as soon as possible. I enlisted in the Army in January of '42, basic training and basic combat training completed at Fort Ord, north of Monterey. Dad had called the state senators from Mono, Inyo, Kern, and San Bernardino Counties, along with the governor to pull stings to get me into OCS. My orders came to report to Officer Candidate School, OCS, at Fort Benning, Georgia.

I graduated after twelve weeks as a Second Lieutenant, went to Military police training and had advanced to the rank of captain in the winter of '44. Commanding Officer of the 44th Military Police Company, I was stationed at RAF, Rattlesden Airfield. The airfield was a few miles southeast of the small village of Bury St Edmonds, Suffolk, England.

I married Harriet Granville shortly after my arrival. She was an only child, and she lived with her elderly parents in the village. Her father was one of the men who made up the village council.

My invitation to tea came two days after my arrival at my new posting.

Harriet was kind enough to show me her parents' property. We toured the main house, the stables, and finally entered the empty caretaker's cottage.

Once inside, she locked the door, stood toe-to-toe with me, and kissed me as if her life depended on us getting together. This girl used her body like a fine racing machine, with speed, agility, and outright power. Before I knew what happened, her guile had trapped me into a marriage. I never had a chance.

Harriet had a way of getting what she thought she wanted. My wife wanted the American Dream—money, a big house, and what passed for happiness. She would get it anyway she could, never caring who had been pushed aside or hurt in her pursuit.

At the time of Harriet's accident, I was at a safety and security meeting up in Bishop.

Every day since then, in my head, I have replayed that note she left me:

Jim,

I've found a man who is willing to take me away from this awful, desolate place.

My true love is Patrick Jensen. He was my history professor at UCLA.

I'm taking Kendall with me.

I am not asking for alimony, all I am asking is that you leave us alone.

Harriet.

Three weeks after her death, I found her diary with her luggage. It had been returned after the crash. In it, Harriet had detailed her childish fantasy about happiness, a fairytale from Victorian times.

Ever since that fateful day, four months ago, my days had blurred into one long continuous loss of consciousness. Drinking cheap

Bourbon most days caused high pitched screeching nightmares, which overshadowed my erratic restless sleep patterns. I was lost in a sea without a shore in sight.

On the day the Hanging Murderer returned, I informed Red that I could not return to work just yet, or possibly never.

Two days after the discovery of the hanged man in the barn, and a week after I bumped into the same man outside the liquor store in Lone Pine, I was in the store again. This time for three bottles of Four Roses, my favorite Kentucky Straight Bourbon Whiskey.

I returned home from my regular trip to the liquor store about eleven in the morning. I had moved back to my parents' ranch house from the bungalow I'd shared with my wife and daughter, the day after their deaths.

Conchita was making lunch on the gas stove in the kitchen. She has worked as a cook and housekeeper at the ranch since she had immigrated from Mexico, years earlier. My mother and Conchita had immediately connected. Conchita was the daughter she never had. Unfortunately, my mother passed away from cancer a year before Harriet and Kendall's deaths.

I felt Conchita's dark chocolate, almond-shaped eyes on me as they bore into my back while I made my way to the leather club chair in the living room My brown paper bag was filled with the bottles of Bourbon.

While I settled into my chair, I took out one bottle, and pulled out the cork stopper before pouring three fingers of the pale caramel colored liquor into my glass tumbler.

I hadn't realized that Conchita followed me into the living room.

'Do you really want to do this?' she asked.

'I don't need your opinion. And there isn't anything else for me to do.'

'Yes, there is, Jim. Stop wallowing in your misery of losing your daughter and Harriet and begin to be the man you are in this town.'

'Who's that, Conchita?'

'A good, decent, honest man, loved by the people of this county.'

'I was only elected because of my father, when he retired as sheriff.'

'No, you misjudge yourself. The county never elected Merrill out of love. They respected him.'

'If that's the case,' I challenged her, 'why have you stayed in this house?'

'I stayed to cook and clean, the job Miss Clara brought me from Mexico to do, when I was a teenager, alone and on my own. If I had stayed in Mexico, I refuse to think what would have become of me.'

Conchita pushed a stray strand of hair behind her ear before she continued. 'I fell in love with your mother. And she confided in me.'

'Confided what?' I demanded. 'I think you know, Jim.'

'That my father had a lot of affairs? Marlene Chambers in particular, at the Sheriff's Office?'

Marlene had been the dispatcher at the sheriff's office for decades. I had inherited her from my father when I was elected sheriff, but I had never liked her. She looked at the little things in life. She didn't take the time in her busy schedule as town gossip to stop and look at a Monarch butterfly flying south to Mexico to survive the cold of winter. No, Marlene's life revolved around who slept with whom last night. After my mother died, I was afraid she was going to worm her way into my father's life.

'So what if my mother knew about my father sparking around with other women?' I told Conchita.

'She felt betrayed by Merrill. If he left your mother for another woman, especially a woman from town, what would people think? The things they would say behind her back were more than she could stand.'

'If you knew my mother so well, what was her plan?'

'I was the plan, Jim.' Conchita's eyes welled up, but she refused to cry. 'Miss Clara and I teamed together to force your father to give up messing around with women in this county.'

I heard Conchita's words and lost myself inside them.

'Miss Clara told him that he was to no longer have any affairs in Inyo County. If he insisted on continuing, then we would make his life a living hell. Miss Clara made it clear, too, if Merrill tried anything with me, she would kill him in his sleep.'

'My mother said that? Good for her.'

'Miss Clara made me promise that if she died from the cancer, I would to be responsible for you.'

'For me?'

'She knew you were unhappy. I knew, too. She didn't trust Harriet. She was always worried for you and for your daughter. And then Mr. Merrill was so lost without her. So here I am, trying to take care of you both.'

Conchita knelt beside me and took my hand in hers. 'The county needs you now, Jim. There are plenty of people here who are waiting for you to come out of this lost time in your life. To face what you were elected to do.' She paused. 'Give up the drinking. Please, do it for your mother and me.'

She rose up and brought her soft lips to mine and kissed me.

The weight of the world fell off my shoulders; I was alive for the first time in years, I wanted with all my heart to kiss her back, but I didn't. It was too sudden, I was still reeling from my losses.

She stood up and went to finish preparing dinner. I filled the tumbler full of Four Roses. I A small sip, just one.

The glass tumbler slipped out of my hand. I didn't want to try to retrieve it. I nodded off.

CHAPTER 9

Merrill was elected sheriff of Inyo County in 1920, a month to the day after his only child, Jim, was born. After Jim was born, Merrill, now sheriff, was busier than a one-armed wallpaper hanger. He never found time to even throw a ball around with the boy. Even without the one-on-one time, Jim idealized his father and grew up wanting to be just like him. Clara was happy with whatever her son wanted to become; she just didn't want him to be a womanizer like Merrill.

Clara had been the glue that held father and son together. Now, it was Conchita. While preparing dinner, she looked over at Jim as he sat scrunched down in the soft leather club chair. A short time later, she heard whiskey glass drop to the floor and she knew he was in a deep sleep.

Conchita tiptoed over to the chair and gazed down at him. She pushed aside a lock of Jim's hair, which had fallen in front of his eyes. She had secretly loved Jim since she had first seen him, when she was nineteen and he had come to the ranch back from England, still in his uniform. She had promised Clara she would take care of him, but today was not a success in her goal to rid the man she loved of his demons and make him whole again.

She went back to the kitchen, not knowing if Jim heard a word she'd said about stopping drinking. The task at hand was making sure dinner was finished and on time for Merrill. He wanted his food on the table as soon as he entered the house and sat down at the table. Tonight, she was making fried chicken exactly like Clara made it, crisp outside, tender, and moist inside.

Alongside the hot chicken, which was drying on some paper towels on the counter, Clara's special riced mashed potatoes with minced garlic and green onions slivers, Merrill's favorite. Last, she had made the chicken gravy, using a roux of butter and flour before adding the chicken broth, stirring constantly to remove any clumps. Conchita took pride in making a meal Clara taught her in this very kitchen. Conchita's eyes welled up.

Merrill finished the repairs to the ranch fences in the early evening. Jim was still asleep in the chair. Merrill picked up the fallen tumbler from the floor next to Jim and threw a woollen camp blanket over his son. Then he went to find out what Conchita was preparing for dinner.

'So, what did my drunken son accomplish today?'

Merrill had been saying things like this about Jim since the tragic deaths of Harriet and Kendall.

Conchita ignored the comment.

She made dinner for Merrill, he always wanted American food. For her own dinner, and Jim's, she made chicken enchiladas with rice, refried beans, and guacamole.

'Merrill, wash up, I'll put your dinner on the table. Then I'll wake Jim up.'

'Is Jim asleep or drunk?'

Not looking at him, Conchita said, 'He fell asleep in the leather chair after he came home from town.'

Skeptical, Merrill asked, 'Did he drink all afternoon?'

'I wasn't watching him; I was making dinner,' Conchita replied.

Conchita quickly put the fried chicken, mashed potatoes and gravy in front of Merrill's place setting, knowing he liked to fix his own plate. She went into the living room to wake Jim.

Leaning down, she gently brushed some of his hair from in front of his eyes as she jiggled his shoulder. 'Jim, it's time to wake up. I made chicken enchiladas the way you like. Please wake up.'

Jim pushed her hand away and growled, 'I want to sleep, leave me alone.' His head slid down to the arm of the chair.

Conchita went to her knees in front of the chair and blew air on his nose. 'It's time to get up, sleepy boy. Dinner.'

Jim opened his eyes, 'Please, Conchita, I just want to sleep, leave me alone.'

Chewing a fried chicken wing, Merrill called out, 'Leave him be, Conchita, come and eat your dinner.'

Before Conchita stood, she kissed Jim on the cheek. Then whispered, 'Jim, come and eat. I don't want to eat alone with your father.'

Jim put his hands under his head and started to snore.

Conchita reluctantly went back to the kitchen, made a small plate of food and sat in Jim's usual place, at the opposite end of the table from Merrill.

Conchita ate small bites, finishing her one enchilada, and pushed her rice and beans around her plate to waste time while not talking. She never lifted her head. Merrill, on the other hand, gobbled a second helping of food before wiping his mouth with his linen napkin and made a muffled burp. Not excusing himself, he then drank a full glass of ice water.

Dinner complete, Merrill took a toothpick from a box from the Lazy Susan in the center of the table and cleaned his teeth. He sat back in his chair, contented as an English nobleman in a grand hall after a feast in the seventeenth century, lit a cigarette and blew the smoke to the celling.

Conchita began to clear the dishes.

'Put aluminum foil over Jim's plate and keep it warm in the oven,' said Merrill.

She fixed the plate without a word. Merrill was about to say something when a blood-curdling scream came from the living room. It froze him in place at the kitchen table. Another, louder, more hideous primal scream rattled the house. He rushed into the living room with Conchita right behind him.

'No, this can't be happening again.' Merrill grabbed his son and held him tight in his arms, not letting him flail around in his semi-asleep state.

Coming to in his father's arms, in a shaking voice, Jim said, 'I saw a crime scene, same as the murders we investigated. The victim was different from the man we saw the other day. Another dead man hanged in another barn.'

'Son, I think you should come to the kitchen and sit down.

Calm yourself and have a glass of water.'

Jim sat at the table, and Conchita placed the warmed plate of food in front of him.

'Jim, your nightmares are all related to your drinking. Son, you need to stop drinking and begin to heal from the deaths of your family.'

Jim said, 'Dad, I have a confession. I never told you that Harriet was taking Kendall leaving me for a professor at UCLA...'

'I don't care what Harriet wanted to do with her life!' Merrill paused. 'Stop drinking or move out.' With that, Merrill left the kitchen.

Conchita busied herself with cleaning up. Jim sat at the kitchen table not touching his food.

After breakfast the next morning, Conchita started to wash the dishes.

Suffering from yesterday's hangover, Jim got up and left the ranch house, got in his truck and drove away.

Merrill went into the den. He sat at his desk, picked up the phone receiver and listened for the phone company's switchboard operator to come on the line. 'Connect me to the sheriff's office. Red Fowler's phone.'

A few seconds passed. 'Hello, this is Acting Sheriff Red Fowler.'

'It's Merrill, and I'm out at the ranch.' 'What's up, Merrill?'

'Jim had a nightmare yesterday afternoon about a Hanging Murder, confusing the murder from 1940 with the dead man the other day.'

'I remember he came out and helped investigate the forty and forty-two murders.'

'I'm worried he's getting worse, Red.'

'That could be the case. What do you suggest?' said Red. 'I'm pushing hm to get back to work but maybe he needs more time off. Another month or two?' Merrill replied. 'Is he still drinking?' Red needed to know.

Sighing, Merrill replied, 'He's pretty bad. '

Red hesitated, then had no choice but to tell Merrill. 'He's expected to return to work on November fifteenth. The county commissioners informed me today he either returns to work or accepts permanent retirement.'

'I understand. I'll talk to him tonight,' Merrill said.

Not one person was ever charged with the Hanging Murders. The sheriff's department never even had a suspect. The police never found out the names of the victims, still referred to as John Doe cases.

Just like then, there were few leads. The California Department of Justice and the FBI worked with the sheriff's department as they shifted through the evidence, which was scant at best.

There were no fingerprints, no tire tracks, or anything on the bodies themselves related to the victims or the killer. There were no witnesses.

The only thing Red was sure of was that if he didn't get Jim back in the office within two weeks, the responsibility of the case would fall squarely on his shoulders. Red shuddered when he thought of that possibility.

CHAPTER 10

It was Friday night, three days after the latest Hanging Murder discovery. The news was still under wraps by order of the FBI and the state DOJ headquarters in Sacramento.

Conchita had dinner ready when Merrill and Jim entered the house. The meal was typical American fare: meatloaf, mashed potatoes, brown gravy, and green beans. The only noise as they were eating came from Merrill chewing his food. Conchita kept her head down, looking at her plate as she pushed her food around.

Dinner finished, all three left for their prearranged assignments. Conchita finished the dishes and went to her room, Merrill talked with Red on the phone about the Hanging Murderer, and Jim was headed to the Cowboy Bar & Grill for a drink. He had his hat in his hand and was slinking out the kitchen door when Conchita came out of her bedroom. She stood leaning against the doorway.

'Don't go out. Don't drink tonight,' she said. 'Stay here with me.'

'I don't think I should,' Jim replied.

Conchita faced him, 'Jim. I'm asking because I've loved you since you arrived at the ranch after the war.'

Jim did a double take when he heard Conchita's revelation. He swallowed before saying, 'I was married then, Conchita. I loved my wife and my daughter.'

'Yes, but Harriet didn't love you. I saw it in her eyes,'

Sadness filled Jim's eyes. 'I wanted her to love me and need me more than anything else.'

There was silence, neither of them speaking as they looked at each other.

Conchita knew what she wanted, she wanted Jim to take her away from this place. She didn't want to make any other decisions. She looked at Jim and couldn't say a word. Her silence spoke volumes.

Shocked and confused, Jim left the house through the back door.

That night she made up her mind what she needed to do.

CHAPTER 11

On Saturday, the Inyo County Sheriff's Office in Independence was awash with FBI and sheriff's department personnel. Red and Merrill were there. It was the fourth day after the Hanging Murder victim's discovery.

They were all working on an outline of the type of suspect or suspects representing a profile of the Hanging Murderer. The Task Force started from the first murder in 1932, through the others: 1934, '37, '40, '42, and the present one, 1957.

The FBI researched the incidents of any other similar murders in all the other western states, and then the rest of the forty-eight. The California state DOJ in Sacramento looked at any murders occurring in California over the same period that were similar

The thirty-man Task Force worked through the late afternoon and into the early evening before breaking up. Red was the last one leaving the conference room when he overheard a couple of FBI agents talking.

The first agent asked, 'Where's Sheriff Cobb?'

The other agent replied, 'Jim Cobb has been under the weather since the sudden death of his wife and daughter on this past 4th of July.'

The FBI agent didn't ask what under the weather meant, but he put his hand to his mouth and acted out the idea of taking a drink. 'Straight Kentucky Bourbon, from the whispers at CHP and any law enforcement people in the Eastern Sierra.'

Red wanted to defend his boss, to punch the FBI agents in the nose. But he uttered not a word to dispute what the agents said. He had respect for his boss as a man and as the sheriff, but even Red could not go on making excuses for the lack of Jim's leadership.

Now with the Task Force in place, there were new people on board. People who didn't know Jim and who were going to make

Inyo County a harder place to work. The big question for Red was, should he tell Jim about what he heard being said behind his back by the agents? Was there a way for Red to get Jim back to work while making it look to others like it was Jim's idea?

CHAPTER 12

On Sunday, Red drove out to Merrill Cobb's ranch. They needed to find out the identity of the latest victim of the Hanging Murderer. Red and Merrill tried cajoling, haranguing, and pleading with Jim about coming back to work.

After a frustrating hour at the kitchen table, Red was tired, he'd had enough of Jim's excuses. Disgusted, he left the ongoing discussion to father and son.

'You were elected to be the sheriff, Jim,' Merrill told his son. 'It is high time you returned to work.'

'That's easy for you to say, Dad. You had your life with Mom. I didn't have that, or time enough with my daughter.'

Merrill tried reasoning with him. 'You're right about time together with loved ones. No one in their right mind would say a negative word about you, or the time you have already spent with your sorrow. I understand, but you need to go back to work'

'I need a little more time,' Jim pleaded.

'No, son, you don't,' Merrill said, trying a different tack. 'The Hanging Murderer is back, and the citizens of Inyo County need your leadership. I couldn't solve it when I was sheriff but you can. I believe in you."

'If you couldn't find the evil bastard who killed five unknown men over ten years, how can I do it?'

'I know you'll find a way.'

'I'll think it over, Dad. I'm going for a ride up to Big Pine.' Jim left the ranch by himself.

Conchita gave Merrill another cup of coffee. 'Your boy will come around and see the need to return to work,' she told him.

'I hope you're right, Conchita.'

Conchita took a deep breath. 'Merrill, I have to leave.' 'Leave? What are you talking about?'

'I have to leave the ranch.'

'No, you don't. Stay and help Jim and me. Where would you go, anyway?'

Sighing, Conchita said, 'Well, I have to clean up the table and do the dishes now.'

Merrill left the house and went out to his woodworking shop in the barn.

Conchita wanted to run after Jim and comfort him, make him safe and secure in her arms. She wanted a life with Jim but it was not going to happen. She knew her days at the ranch were over. Moving in with her sister and their family was her only answer to keep her heart from breaking on a daily basis.

Conchita whispered a prayer. 'God, if you hear me, I have only one wish. Please let me have a life with Jim Cobb.'

CHAPTER 13

On Tuesday morning, seven days after the discovery of the latest Hanging Murder, the medical examiner drove up from Los Angeles County, since Inyo County was too small in population to have a full-time medical examiner. The sheriff, in sparsely populated counties in California, was the elected county coroner, too, but it did not warrant the job title of medical examiner.

The autopsy was conducted at ten a.m. at the Lone Pine Funeral Home by Mark Crawley and was completed by noon. Crawley, on the short side of forty, was brash, full of himself, a doctor who acted as if his findings in any death were the last word. Jim Cobb couldn't stand the man and would never become friends with him.

The official report detailed the following:

The external exam revealed a white male, approximately thirty to thirty-five years of age, thin, to the point of undernourished, weight one hundred fifty-two pounds, seventy-two inches in length, eye color blue (petechial hemorrhaging in the sclera's of each eye), hair color light brown. There were no birthmarks, and an old scar started below the left eye and jaggedly continued to the side of the nose, no moles, or tattoos.

A large incision starting from outside the right external jugular vein, transecting the jugular vein and right common carotid artery, right and left sternocleidomastoid muscles, platysma muscle, left common carotid artery, the left external jugular vein partially transected indicating the assailant was left-handed. (The incision was performed while the body was hung upside down.)

There was also an anterior incision across the trachea. The face and head superior to the incision line had darkened from lividity turning the tissues a blackish color. The internal exam was unremarkable except for the fracturing of the hyoid bone in the neck indicating the victim was asphyxiated from hanging before the neck incision.

X-rays of the victim were taken and showed the results of two fractures of cervical vertebra, C-1, and C-2. There was also an incidental X-ray finding, a previous broken left forearm, approximately fifteen years before death. The brain exam was also unremarkable. The organs were replaced inside the body cavity and the skin sewn back in place.

The official cause of death was asphyxiation from hanging, a broken neck (cervical vertebra, C-1, and C-2), a broken hyoid bone, and almost complete exsanguination, also, petechial hemorrhaging in the sclera's of each eye indicating asphyxiation.

Fingerprints of the victim revealed no match in the State system to his identity. The FBI sent a copy of them to their lab at Marine Corps Base Quantico, which had opened in November of 1932.

The state DOJ went through case studies for any other murders which could lead to any clues to the identity of the victim and the other unknown victims between 1932 and 1942.

Red sent out sheriff deputies to all corners of the county to find anyone who could give any information about this latest murder victim.

Grady Bennett wrote a story about the Hanging Murders, which ran in the *LA Post* in the next day's edition and was culled from information supplied by Edith and an interview with Red Fowler, done the day before the autopsy. In it, Grady recapped all the information concerning all the previous John Doe Hanging Murders. He noted that the Inyo County Sheriff's Office, the FBI, and state DOJ were all on the case.

Grady thought the story was what he needed to propel him to a better position at the newspaper, one with more prestige.

A threat on his life was the last thing he thought would occur.

CHAPTER 14

Grady was getting tired of Lone Pine. He had made himself comfortable at Edith's house. The sex was great, but there wasn't much for him to do during the day while she was at work, except write his take on the Hanging Murderer. He needed something to happen.

Grady called his editor, Sid Haber, at the LA Post. 'The head honcho wants you to stay in Lone Pine for whatever possible follow-up there is on this murder case.' Sid told him.

'Okay, Sid I'll hang around. Talk to you in a few days.'

The first thing he wanted to do was try again to interview Barton Haskel. But there was no sign of Barton as of Wednesday. The man was last seen the previous Friday night. He had been working at the Cowboy Bar & Grill when Grady and Edith had left that night around midnight.

His next plan was to interview the sheriff. When Grady asked Edith how to get in touch with Jim Cobb, she told him what Red had confided in her—that Jim wasn't ready to return to work.

Grady was at Edith's house reading the newspaper that afternoon when the phone rang. Grady answered, thinking it was her. 'Hello, beautiful.'

'This is not about that whore you're sleeping with,' the caller said. 'I'm telling you, for your own good, Bennett, stop writing stories about the Hanging Murders, or else your life isn't worth a hill of beans.'

'What? Who is this?' He heard a click. 'Hello, hello?' The line was dead.

At first, he thought the call was from some crackpot in LA. He decided to call his editor. 'Sid, did anyone in Los Angeles ask for the phone number in Lone Pine where I'm staying? Who knows I'm not at the hotel?'

'No one here. But I'll ask around,'

Grady called Edith at the sheriff's office and asked her the same question.

'No one in town even knows where you're staying. No one has called the sheriff's office for you, either. Why?'

'Don't worry about it, thanks, beautiful.' Grady hung up.

Edith blushed. A warm feeling rose up inside her. Giggling over her java in the sheriff's office, she had told them about her new love. She did not put two and two together about what she had whispered to coworkers during the last three days.

CHAPTER 15

On Thursday, ten days after the newest Hanging Murder victim, Grady Bennett's article was picked up and printed on the front page of the *Modesto Sentinel*. A copy of the paper sat on the kitchen table in a small one-bedroom apartment shared by Archie Reid and his girlfriend, Gretchen. Her hair tied in a ponytail, she was making fried pork chops for dinner.

In Modesto, the Di Rosa winery was the major employer in the thriving agricultural community and that's where Archie worked, driving a long-haul truck for the winery. Archie was a lanky six feet tall, with dark hair and pale blue eyes, like the color of ice in a winter stream. He and Gretchen met at the annual company Wine Harvest picnic in September 1950.

Gretchen was a determined young woman, five-five, with black hair, hazel eyes, and an athletic body made for dancing. When they met, she was a lively eighteen-year-old who had just graduated from Modesto High School. She was also smart as a whip. She wanted to run the winery someday and started her climb to success in the bottling plant.

The couple moved in together, two years after they met, Archie had told Gretchen all about his life growing up in Inyo County, secrets he had never told anybody except one Army buddy.

Archie spied the headline in the newspaper on the table: 'Hanging Murderer Returns After 15 Years.' Anxiety instantly overtook Archie. He went over to where Gretchen was standing at the stove, the newspaper in his hand. 'Honey, I need to return to Lone Pine.'

She saw the headline and understood why Archie had to leave. The fear of the unknown, washed over her like a rogue wave in the ocean. Gretchen knew she must be strong for her man. 'Are you going to call your Army buddy?'

'I will,' he replied, picking up the phone. 'Reinhard, I read an article about the Hanging Murderer and his return after fifteen years to Lone Pine.'

'I read the same article in the Chicago paper,' came the response.

Archie, twenty-eight, was Silas and Minerva Reid's only child. The Reids had lived in Inyo County since 1931. Archie enlisted in the Army in April of 1942, and the first man he met in the service was Reinhard Diefenbach. Reinhard joined at eighteen, too, his height of six feet two inches reflected his lanky stature, with long arms and broad shoulders.

He and Archie could have almost been twins and they became fast friends from that day onward. Each man would lay down their life to save the other. They were better than friends, they were brothers, stronger than if they had the same mother. Both men were raised in conservative families, and were grown men who didn't cry or show outward affection.

Both had volunteered to join the Airborne Infantry. They arrived in Toccoa, Georgia in November 1942 with the 501st Parachute Infantry Regiment. Together, they went to basic infantry training and in May 1943, they earned their jump wings at Fort Benning, Georgia.

Shortly after jump school and throughout the summer, the regiment undertook company, battalion, and regimental training at Camp McCall, North Carolina, and participated in the Tennessee maneuvers.

The 501st PIR, commanded by Col. Howard Johnson (Jumpy Johnson), was attached to the 101st Airborne Division, the Screaming Eagles, just before the regiment departed for England in December of 1943.

They made their first combat jump at Normandy shortly after midnight, the morning of June 6, 1944, D-Day.

The two friends fought side-by-side throughout Europe without so much as a scratch.

Archie never talked openly about his family back in California. He was quiet and hesitant about them; he told Reinhard that his father was dead.

Reinhard knew from his own family that secrets were buried deep within the family tree. Some people's names changed when they came through Ellis Island, others had 'black sheep' or silent relatives. Then there were those who had familial history so unspeakable, they never uttered a word. Reinhard instinctively knew this last situation was Archie's family.

Christmas 1944, the two buddies were huddled in a cold foxhole outside the Belgian town of Bastogne during the Battle of the Bulge. The foxhole was covered with pine boughs and some boards the men had managed to scrounge from bombed out buildings nearby.

Archie slept like the dead, but that night, he talked out loud about things he never divulged while awake. While Archie was sleeping, Reinhard heard bits and pieces of the story his best friend told in his sleep. The tale of the Hanging Murderer of Inyo County.

At first, Reinhard had thought what he was hearing was just a nightmare, created by an over-imaginative mind under duress during wartime. He would have believed that, if the sleep-talking had stopped after one night, but it didn't. Archie relived it over the next three nights the two men survived in that foxhole. Each night he gave more gruesome details. His fear of his father was palpable. Reinhard knew his friend would need his help to get past the nightly torment he suffered.

Archie never returned to his parents' ranch after the war, and he had never written to his father, not even a postcard. He had sent a birthday card to his mother after returning to the United States in November, six months after V-E Day in 1945. In the card, he'd said that he was alive and well, and he was making a life for himself. He did not tell her where he was living, never mentioning whether he would ever see her again.

Together, they returned to the USA in November 1945 to be discharged. Archie roamed around the country alone until landing in Modesto.

Reinhard returned to Chicago and worked at Diefenbach's German Delicatessen, his family's business. When he read the article in the *Chicago Examiner* about the Hanging Murderer he knew this had to do with his best friend. Reinhard was ready when Archie called. 'I'll meet you in Lone Pine at the bus station the day after tomorrow.

CHAPTER 16

The final autopsy report was sent to the sheriff's office on Friday, November 1, ten days after the discovery of the murder victim. Red Fowler looked it over. It read like all the other Hanging Murder autopsies he'd seen.

There was no identification of the deceased. The victim was a six-foot tall white male, approximately thirty to thirty-five years of age, light brown hair, blue eyes, weight, one hundred fifty-two pounds. A jagged scar started below the left eye and went to his nose, and there were no birthmarks or tattoos. The victim did have a previous broken left forearm, and the incident took place approximately fifteen years before death.

The cause of death was asphyxiation due to hanging, with fractures of C-1 and C-2 and the hyoid bone. A hesitation laceration preceded a deep incision across the anterior neck from right carotid to left, causing almost complete exsanguination. That caught Red's attention. The laceration was one and a half inches in depth, and nine inches in length, both common carotid arteries, internal and external jugular veins were all completely severed. The incision started from right to left, indicating a left-handed individual made the cut. The neck laceration occurred within minutes of death.

The remaining blood in the body settled, due to lividity, in the face and head causing the superficial tissue to look blackish. Red already knew that the death occurred approximately sixty to seventy hours before the discovery of the body, time reached due to the lack of rigor mortis.

There were no leads, no person who was a likely suspect. The state DOJ and FBI had little useful information. They were working around the clock on the case, contacting the surrounding areas and states for anything useful.

When Red called Merrill to discuss the information and try to get Jim back in the office. asked, 'Is he ready to come back yet?'

'No. Jim had a bad night and drank himself into a stupor.' Merrill sighed. 'We argued this morning, and he has no interest in returning to work.'

'Damnit,' Red growled. 'Where is he now?'

'He left the house this morning, said he was driving out into the hills. I don't know where.'

'Thanks, Merrill. Down at the station, we're all stumped, just like we were with the first five murders. We sure could use a fresh set of eyes to get us headed in the right direction.'

'I'll tell him when he returns.'

CHAPTER 17

A movie location director and his assistant from London, England, were sent to the states for Trident Pictures. They were looking for unique locations for a science fiction drama. The production company planned to start with the outdoor scenes. Filming was to begin in January, so they needed to find a location quickly.

They were in a Jeep, driving around the Lone Pine area. The two men were at the Movie Flats, in the Alabama Hills Recreation area. Their ride was taking them along Movie Road to the sight of the Gunga Din Bridge, named after the 1939 movie starring Cary Grant and Douglas Fairbanks, Jr.

The men hadn't seen any other cars driving on the hard dirt and gravel road, not a single person, since they had left the town of Lone Pine. When they turned to see the bridge area, the assistant spotted a single car parked off the road, about 500 yards away.

Reggie said, 'Mr. Donaldson, that's a 1941 Buick Estate Wagon. A Woody. Look. Rich maroon color with real tan colored cloth interior, split front windshield, rear fender skirts, and a barrel roof. I came out to California in 1949 to visit my namesake Uncle in Pasadena. Uncle Reggie had a car exactly like this one. He let me drive it out to Santa Monica. It was a jolly good time.'

But the Woody, pointing away from the road and sitting alone, seemed odd. They drove to within thirty feet of the vehicle.

The director stopped the jeep and called out in his thick English accent. 'Hello, anyone there?' He waited a few moments before calling again. 'I say, sir, is everything all right?'

Standing outside their Jeep, the two waited for a response. When none came, the director said, 'Reggie, go and see what that bugger is doing. Be jolly quick about it. We have locations to view.'

'Yes, Mister Donaldson, I'll be right back.'

Reggie walked up to the back of the car from the passenger side and saw what looked like someone sitting in the driver's seat. As he walked closer, he called, 'Hello there, you, in the car. Do you need any help? Can we be of assistance?'

Reggie went around the trunk, towards the driver's door. He looked through the closed window and saw the man's face staring back at him with his head resting on the steering wheel. The man's eyes were open but clouded over with a blank, milky stare.

Reggie screamed, 'Oh, God, blimey, he's dead!' He pointed to the body with one shaking hand and covered his mouth with the other as he kept screaming.

Donaldson ran to the side of the car to have a look. He had served in the British army during the war in Burma, and he'd seen death many times. 'Stop it!' He ordered and grabbed Reggie's shoulders, shaking him.

Reggie pointed, his voice breaking. 'Is he dead, Mr. Donaldson?'

'It looks like it. Go back and sit in the Jeep. Calm down. I'll look around. Go on, now.'

Reggie trotted back to the Jeep as Donaldson walked around the sedan. The car was locked tight, with only the one individual in the car. Donaldson could see that the dead man had a revolver in his right hand.

Donaldson and Reggie drove back the way they came. The first building they came upon was a Union 76 gas station. They stopped and Donaldson called the sheriff's office. The two Englishmen couldn't imagine the hornets' nest they had just stirred up with their early morning discovery.

A deputy, Bob Roth, was sent from the Lone Pine patrol division to see what the 'city fellows' had found. Deputy Roth met the foreigners at the gas station and followed them to the location of the car with the dead man inside.

The day was Friday, ten days since the discovery of the latest Hanging Murder victim in the barn at the old Conroy Ranch.

CHAPTER 18

Deputy Carl Swanson was staffing the dispatch two-way phone system while Marlene Chambers was on her morning break. He suddenly bolted out of the enclosed area set aside for the dispatcher and ran directly into Edith Pearson. He stopped to speak quietly to her.

Edith let out a high pitched, ear shattering scream. 'Noooooooo, it can't be!' Edith cried and then fainted in the arms of the deputy.

Red was on the phone with his cousin, Theo Culpepper, when Edith screamed.

'I'll call you back after I find out what just happened in the office.' He dropped the phone into its cradle and went out to the open area of the office.

Edith was now sitting in a chair and Carl was holding a glass of water for her. She was taking deep breathes, with her head down.

'What the hell just happened?' demanded Red.

'I was working the dispatch line, Chief. Bob Roth from the Lone Pine patrol division called on the two-way from the crime scene. You know, where the two Limeys phoned in about this morning. The car is a 1942 Buick Estate Wagon, a Woody, with real wood siding. The exact same car Barton bought in San Bernardino in 1944 off a used car lot for four-hundred dollars.'

'What did he report?'

'The body he found at the Gunga Din bridge was Barton Haskel.' Carl looked stricken, but continued, 'He says it looks like a suicide.'

Red's life took a nosedive with the latest news. Inyo County now had another questionable death within two weeks and this latest one was a retired deputy sheriff and prominent Lone Pine business owner.

Red didn't know what to do first: call Jim to take over? Help Edith recover from her fainting spell? Or go back in his office and hide from all the ruckus.

This latest situation made Red want nothing more than to retire and go trout fishing up at Silver Lake, where his family had had a cabin for many years, since the actor, Wallace Berry, had settled in the pristine woodsy hideaway in the 1920s

CHAPTER 19

I'll keep working on the Hanging Murders, looking for any new leads. Talk to you in a few days,' Grady said to his editor, hung up the phone and was starting to make another call when he heard a noise at the front door.

The door opened and Edith stumbled in unexpectedly, looking dazed. Deputy Roth brought her home, saw her to the door, and drove off. She dropped her bag on the floor, and fell into Grady's arms. He picked her up and took her into the bedroom. Laying her down on the bed, he removed her shoes, and placed a wet washcloth on her forehead. Worried, he sat rubbing her hands, wishing she would tell him what was wrong.

A few minutes later, Grady began to get frantic. He didn't know a goddamn thing about first aid. What should he do? Call the police or his editor at the paper? If Edith dies…

Fear contracted his body.

Grady put another wet washcloth on Edith's head. He stopped rubbing her hands and moved to gently rubbing her face, calling in a louder voice, 'Edith, wake up! Tell me what happened! I see your chest moving up and down, so your breathing,' Grady's frantic questions were creating sweat on his forehead as he shouted at her, 'Edith! You're scaring me!'

Edith started to come around, but she could barely speak. 'Barton Haskel's dead,' she gasped. 'Two men found him out at the Movie Flats this morning.' She managed to say this before breaking down and crying in Grady's arms.

'Dead?' Grady's mind started working overtime, 'How did he die?'

After a few minutes she was able to tell him the entire story. Although Grady knew Edith needed him, he went into reporter mode, a second

death in the little community of Lone Pine within two weeks. His mind was whirling with every
conceivable outcome to the new death and the other murder.

Edith looked at him. 'I need to tell you something.'

'What is it, love?' Grady asked, as he worked his way around the room gathering his notepad and some pencils. He placed the items in the outside pocket of his jacket and went to the door. He had his hand on the doorknob.

'Barton and I were lovers right after I started working at the sheriff's office.' Her words came fast as she rushed to get it all out. 'The affair ended when he fell in love with Lara Aartz. Her father was the assistant ambassador to the United States from the Netherlands before he retired. They would meet in secret in San Diego.'

'Was he still seeing her?' he asked, as his hand fell from the doorknob.

'He would have told me if he wasn't.'

Grady knew about Edith's affair with Barton from the first night they met at the Cowboy Bar & Grill, but he hadn't heard anything about a Miss Lara Aartz. He had a vague recollection of Johannes Van Aartz being in the news when the retired assistant ambassador from the Netherlands had chosen to live in San Diego.

This new wrinkle heated up the journalistic juices in Grady's head. He realized he would learn more about Barton by staying and comforting Edith after the shock of his death.

The news about Lara Aartz had his senses flowing as the thread of a story began to germinate in his brain. The rich, only daughter of the retired, widowed assistant ambassador from the Netherlands made great flash-in-the-pan society news with the ne'er-do-well-wannabes of L.A., but Grady wanted the story behind the gossip. How did Lara get involved with a deputy sheriff from the wilds of Inyo County? Did he kill himself because she rejected him? What was the real story?

Grady's nose twitched as a warmth of anticipation coursed through his body. The urge of the story was taking over, and nothing was going to stop him from grabbing the gold ring. This sensation, for Grady, was better than sex.

CHAPTER 20

The temperature for late October was still in the high nineties. The old, faded Chevy pickup was a little west of Needles, California. The grizzled man, his two-day-old beard, mostly gray in color, drove the truck at about fifty miles per hour

He was looking for a place to eat lunch, and maybe find a cheap woman to satisfy his needs. He parked the truck outside a dusty little restaurant, one frequented by long-haul truckers traveling along Route 66. It was an okay place to eat. It was a better place to find a woman who wanted to make a few bucks.

While eating, he asked a few of the drivers if they knew of a place for what he had in mind. He didn't get the desired response before leaving the restaurant.

The truck was headed south along the Arizona border when the man saw a woman walking down the road. He thought she could be Mexican, maybe Indian, maybe mixed. Smiling at the exotic idea, he slowed the truck and watched her. She was carrying a bundle on her head, holding on with one hand and counterbalancing with the other hand on her hip.

The afternoon heat was oppressive when he stopped next to the woman, who looked about thirty-five, maybe forty.

She was dusty from the blowing dirt along the road, her face tired. The sweat mixed with dirt to make dark areas under her eyes. The man knew she was younger than he originally thought, the wind, heat, and hard work making her appear older.

She didn't want a ride but relented after the man gave her some water from a soda bottle he'd filled at the restaurant. He placed her belongings in the bed of his truck and drove down the empty road with the windows down, allowing a hot breeze to wash over them.

The woman didn't speak. Pointing, she directed him to turn off Route 66 onto a dirt track which lead out into the empty desert.

A couple of miles from the main road, the pair came upon a windowless, one room adobe shack with a tin roof. A few chickens clucked as they scratched for food in the dirt.

The man stopped the truck and brought the woman's belongings into the house as he followed her over the threshold. The adobe shack was cool and dark. The only light entered from the still open doorway.

The woman babbled in Spanish, or Indian, or both, thanking the man for his help in bringing her home. She wanted him gone before her man returned from work. Her man would come home soon and if he found the gringo in his house there would be trouble. But he was not leaving, and she became frightened.

He laughed, then backhanded her with a loud slap. She didn't say another word, just gave in to him as he ripped the clothes from her body.

She cried once, when he was finished, the tears rolling down her face, leaving dirt streaks behind. She wanted to cover her nakedness.

The woman heard someone running up to the house. The light from the doorway was blocked as her man came through the door. Rage filled his eyes when he saw his woman on the floor, holding a torn dress over her naked body. He stopped and knelt before her. 'Who the hell did this to you?' He looked around for the cause of his woman's shame.

Suddenly, a knife plunged into his abdomen and pulled up towards his heart. His entrails fell to the floor before his dead body crumbled down. The woman's eyes grew wide as she realized she was next.

The man left them on the floor in their own blood, returning to his truck. He headed to the border. Driving south, he whistled a tune he'd heard when visiting Albuquerque, the year before. The man thought life was good, independent, and free. He could do whatever he wanted to anyone who came along.

The power the man experienced after a kill made him feel superior and empowered. He was righteous in the eyes of the Lord when it came to setting things right, where white dominance prevailed.

CHAPTER 21

It was a little after one in the afternoon and I had just finished the lunch Conchita had prepared. Her variation of chicken enchiladas, rice, and refried beans was one of my favorite dishes. My thoughts meandered to a couple of double Bourbons, neat, before the afternoon sun made the rest of the day too warm to enjoy any alcohol.

The phone rang out in the living room and I went to answer it while Conchita started clearing the dishes.

'Merrill, is that you?'

'No, he hasn't come in for lunch yet. This is Jim.'

'Jim, this is Marlene, down at the office.' She sounded distraught. 'I need to reach your daddy. There is terrible news.'

'Calm down now, Marlene, and tell me what happened. I will relay any news you have to my father when he comes in.'

Marlene took a deep breath. 'Barton Haskel is dead, Jim.'

It was like a bolt of lightning hit me square in the chest. I wanted to ask a million questions, which flooded my brain instantly. Before I could respond she kept talking.

'Barton was found in his locked car, out in the Alabama Hills area by two movie location scouts. A deputy went out to the location and radioed back, telling us that it looked like Barton.' The line seemed to go dead, then Marlene said, 'The deputy said it looks like he committed suicide.'

The news of Barton's death shook my world, but the idea it was a suicide didn't make any sense.

'I'll give the news to my father, Marlene.' Unable to talk anymore, I hung up, collapsing into the club chair. I felt like a prizefighter hit by a knockout punch. One who wasn't revived until after the ten count.

Barton Haskel was the best senior mentor a young rookie ever came across. He took me under his wing when I joined the sheriff's department, just after my 20th birthday, when I was back from the war. I was going to follow in Dad's footsteps. The person I loved more than anyone else.

I was assigned to Barton as my trainer my first day on the job. He told me that Merrill wouldn't abide by any rudeness to the public, laziness on the job, or any deputy not knowing the letter of the law. Any mistakes to these rules, by anyone, was unacceptable. That day, and he told me from the get-go that Merrill was hard, tough, but fair to every man in the department.

Learning of Barton's death, and his possible suicide, hit me almost as hard as the loss of Kendall. I was mad if he did it and angrier if someone else did it to him. If it was the latter, then I was going to catch the fucking bastard who put my closest friend in the ground.

As I took a shower, I thought about how Barton had acted all rough, hard, and standoffish, but after I started riding in the patrol car, he told me that working in the sheriff's office was the best job he'd ever had in his life. Barton and I rode throughout the county acting like Wyatt Earp and his brother Morgan, the law enforcers who ruled over Tombstone, Arizona. Everything we did together was like a movie, good against evil, and we were the men who wore the white hats and carried the silver badges.

One time, it was early in 1941, I hadn't turned twenty-one yet, Barton and I had to take a wanted prisoner back to the jail in Tijuana.

After we dropped off the prisoner, Barton took me to several cantinas in the old part of town. We drank shots of tequila until I almost couldn't stand upright. Then he pointed out the most beautiful woman I had ever seen, at least I thought so, in my drunken state.

Her hair was down to her shoulders, black and silky, lipstick was ruby red. The dress she wore was cut low over the top of her breasts. She wore red high heels, and a slit went up the side of her dress, almost up to the waist.

She stood next me at the bar, and her head barely reached my shoulder even with heels on. Dark chocolate eyes bore into my soul as she flicked her long lashes. When she did speak, her voice was like a morning wake-up voice, smoky around the edges. She was naughty, wicked, and aroused a place deep inside me that I didn't even know existed. Looking at her face, I couldn't speak a word, but was bewitched by the spell she cast upon me. She smelled like vanilla. She took my hand and led me to a secluded room, way in the back of the bar, apart from any others.

In the morning, Amparo kissed me awake.

I made my way through the warren of rooms back to the cantina in a fog. A couple of ancianas, old women, were cleaning up the bar with mops, airing out the stale air from the smoke and beer of the night before. The dark room made navigating between tables and chairs daunting. I looked up and saw Barton in the open doorway, leaning against the jam, with a yard-wide smile on his face.

'How about some breakfast, buckaroo?'

I got out of the shower and started shaving off my stubble, thinking about when I left Lone Pine for my commission in the army in '43, and my dad and I shook hands as I put my foot on the first step before getting on the train, he said, 'Jim, remember when you and Barton took the prisoner back to Tijuana? Remember that woman you spent the night with behind the cantina? You thought she fell for you? Barton bought you that prostitute.'

He laughed at me like it was the best damn joke he ever heard. He started walking back to town still, laughing about me. I boarded the train hearing that man's humiliating laugh as I went off to war.

I finished shaving, wiped off any excess shaving cream, combed my hair down flat and remembered how much I've hated and loved my father at the same time.

I called Red, my other mentor, from the living room phone. 'I want my job back.'

Red didn't ask me if I was drinking.

I offered, 'I'm now on the wagon, and I will not have another drink until I find Barton Haskel's killer.' I hung up. The room was as silent as an empty church.

I knew that when my dad heard the news, he would be happy I was returning to work. My other thoughts went to Conchita. She, too, was happy.

Who killed Barton? It wasn't suicide, that's one thing I was sure of. Was there a connection between Barton's killer and the Hanging Murders?

I was jumping back into the fire, ready, willing, and hopefully able to take on any obstructions in my way. I had purpose again, throwing off all the chains I'd wrapped around me since the deaths of Kendall and Harriet. Looking backwards and living in the past was over for good. I was turning a corner in my life and nothing was going to stop me from reaching my goal—to find and convict the man or men who had killed Barton Haskel.

CHAPTER 22

I read the report written by Bob Roth, the deputy who was first on the scene with the two English movie location directors. The body was found in was a 1941 Buick Estate Wagon, a Woody, maroon color with tan interior. I knew in my soul this was Barton's car.

The information: Barton Haskel, forty-eight-years-old, a single gunshot wound entering his right temple and exiting the left side of his head. A .38 caliber Smith & Wesson Special revolver (presumed to be the service revolver belonging to Barton Haskel) was found in the right hand of the deceased. A handwritten note was on the passenger's seat.

The note was handwritten, presumably by Barton. It said that he was involved with the serial Hanging Murders and that he was the master robber who had been stealing from the movie community for more than twenty years. I didn't believe Barton could be a murderer, but a thief was a horse of a different color.

I had to do some serious soul searching about Barton's death. Was this really a suicide? My gut told me no way. How to go about finding his killer? Or killers?

Who wanted him dead? Who had the means, motive, and opportunity to kill Barton Haskel?

The last time Barton was seen alive was Friday night into Saturday morning at the Cowboy. He probably closed by himself. I'd check with Juan. So my guess was that Barton had to be taken by someone or several people the last night he was at the Cowboy Bar & Grill. Or it could have happened Saturday morning at his house.

Who were his kidnappers and where was he taken?

Who was the real Barton Haskel? Was Barton in reality a thief? A murderer?

If Barton was a thief, what did he do with the stolen goods?

If Barton was a murderer, did he work alone or have an accomplice? No, impossible. Barton was not a murderer.

That brought me back to the Hanging Murders. What started the killing? Where, when, for how long?

I realized that there was no time like the present to start my journey to find out the truth.

The only good thing about this day was that I had a reason to be back on the job, something I never would have expected. The death of your best friend, or who you imagined to be your best friend, was a reason to make anyone wake up from a nightmare and see the early light of day.

Thoughts kept racing through my mind:

Do we really know anyone? Who they are, and what do they think?

Do we pass others without noticing who they are?

When I was drinking, none of these thoughts entered my head. I was in love with being in a daze, sliding through each day without a care. No questions asked or answered, no involvement with others, and no connections to the world. What a life it is when the only thing on your mind is the next drink. Pathetic was the only answer I had for the last four months.

I told my dad and Red, 'I know you've both lost confidence in me over the last four months, with my wallowing in self-pity.' I stood up. 'Gentlemen, I will find the bastards who committed these murders.'

Merrill's face lit up with pride, knowing a Cobb was back in charge of Inyo County.

Red rose and shook my hand. 'I've been waiting for you to return to work for the last four months. Glad you're back on board, Jim.'

We all left my office with a new purpose. Justice had turned a corner, and nothing was going to come in its way until the job was done. I was walking with a new resolve, no longer with Bourbon as my crutch.

The need to reach down into my soul and find the mechanism that forced me to succeed when all else seemed dark and unattainable was growing inside me. My goal was winning, always winning, never accepting the possibility of defeat. I didn't know what drove me over the finish line, but I knew that not finishing was not an option.

My driving force, some might say, was handed down from my father. But after hearing from Conchita about my mother, I knew differently. The force to be successful came from my mom. She didn't take lemons and make lemonade, she looked at wanton deceit and turned it visually in the community to a happily married life. The resulting outcome was my mother won, my father lost inside Inyo County, and the town won with the lack of gossip dealing with the backdoor love life of the county sheriff.

As I turned the events of the last thirteen years in my parent's home around and looked at all the hurt inflicted, I realized that just winning was not the answer. People needed to walk with their heads held high and to go beyond just surviving. I needed to. It was three days after Barton's body was found, alone in his car out in the Alabama Hills, that I stood next to the medical examiner as he performed the autopsy in the basement of the Lone Pine Funeral Home. The room had that bitter, alcohol smell I remembered from the doctor's office. I hated it. Every time I came to one of these autopsies, the smell was there, overpowering and pervasive. I put some camphor gel under my nose so I could get through the ripe odor of death and the room's antiseptic stench.

I'd stopped drinking, using grit and determination, without thinking about the withdrawal symptoms caused by the sudden cessation of alcohol consumption. I willed myself to not have the DTs I had witnessed first-hand in England while I was in the Army. Still, I was on my own. There were no handbooks on the subject or any people to talk to about my problem. Instead, to get through it, I focused on the end of the line, Barton's murder.

My present thoughts didn't get muddled by my physical condition but centered on my questions:

What did you do, Barton?

More importantly, why did you do it?

Everyone I talked with thought my friend had put a single bullet from his .38 Smith & Wesson into his right temple while he sat in his car out at the Alabama Hills filming location.

The medical examiner, Dr. Crawley, told me, 'The gun was still in Barton's right hand when his body was found. This indicates that Barton was the shooter. Gunshot residue was found on his hand and arm.'

Crawley continued, 'Barton died instantly. The single gunshot, with a starburst pattern of splitting the skin around the wound, occurs when the gun is pressed against the skin over bone. There's no place for the gas that's exploding out the gun, so it explodes under the skin and creates a stellate pattern. The bullet traversed Barton's right temple, then at a forty-five-degree angle upward and across into his upper parietal lobe on the left side of his head. A single bullet was recovered, flattened, but intact, from above his head in the car's roof panel. The ballistic techs at the DOJ Laboratory have the gun and bullet for scientific comparison.'

I accumulated all the information given to me by Crawley, ran the results through my brain and said, 'Barton was left-handed when it came to shooting, a righty for everything else.'

I paused to let this news settle. 'The local school forced Barton to write with his right hand or get his hands rapped with a ruler. Barton learned to use his right hand, but when he joined the sheriff's department, he always shot his weapon using his left hand.'

'Is there anyone else in the sheriff's office who can corroborate this?'

'Everyone who went to the shooting range with Barton. We all knew he always shot his weapon with his left hand.' I stood there, stone cold sober. 'Barton's death was a murder, not a suicide. Period. End of discussion, Doctor.'

With that, I turned and exited out of the autopsy room. My mission was clear. Find Barton Haskel's murderer or die trying.

CHAPTER 24

Driving south to the border with Mexico and inland from Arizona, one comes to the Imperial Valley, between the Sultan Sea and the Colorado River. A fertile land filled with the unique culture of the area, people of the United States and Mexico. The biggest city is El Centro, home to a little over 10,000 people. It sits twelve miles north of the border town of Calexico on the U.S. side and Mexicali on the Mexican side.

A lone woman was leaving a hole in the wall bar located on the edge of El Centro. She was no more than eighteen or nineteen and had a black leather purse which hung around her neck, and flat shoes with scuff marks. At 11 p.m., the temperature was still in the nineties. She was tired from the heat. Another score from a john would help her buy groceries for her infant daughter and ancient grandmother. The baby's father had left for Mexico a week ago, looking for work.

The old Chevy pickup, with the older man driving, eased up next to the woman. The man in the truck spoke the few words he knew in what he called Mexican. He never knew Mexican wasn't a language, that he was speaking Spanish. The way he figured, French people spoke French, Italians spoke Italian, Mexicans spoke Mexican. He practiced, hello, thank you, you're pretty, and what he understood for intercourse. He rattled off these words through the open side window to the woman, she got in, and they drove off. The woman didn't really understand what the man was saying, but his body language sealed the deal.

He drove to a deserted road outside of town and parked far enough away from the main road so that any passing cars would not see where he had stopped. It lasted all of twenty minutes. It wasn't good or bad, just the age-old ritual of what a man and a woman did. What they were intended to do since the Garden of Eden so long ago.

They adjusted their clothes, the man offered the woman a drink from his Tequila bottle. They both took long gulps without wiping the mouth of the bottle before they drank, each letting the raw strong taste burn down their throats. It was cheap Tequila. The drink let them forget the night and the last twenty minutes.

It was nearing midnight. It was hot in the truck and smelled of sweat and sex. The man pulled money out of his pocket, peeling off a five-dollar bill and handed it over to her. She nodded her appreciation and added her wages to her other money in her purse.

As she put away her money, the man placed his coarse hand over her mouth. She tried to scream; her eyes wild with fear. He pushed a knife into her side above her skirt, watching her face as she realized that her life was ending. She imagined her baby girl growing up without a mother.

The woman never made a sound as she slumped against the door, her eyes closed like she was dreaming and not dead. The man drove his truck back to the main road, over the ruts and potholes, as he kept the knife in place with his right hand. He stopped his truck about fifteen yards from the main road and parked just off to the side.

He leaned over the woman, grabbed the purse she still held in her hand with her earnings from the night, and opened the passenger side door while his hand still held onto the knife. The lifeless body fell out of the truck as the man pulled out his knife. He wiped off her blood on his pant leg and drove his truck south to Mexicali for a place to sleep and then to get some breakfast.

The man in the pickup truck didn't give a damn who he killed, a man, woman, young, old, white, Mexican. His mind told him when he needed to kill. He went on his way doing what he did, not talking about it. He had no friends so there was no need to talk with others. He drove around alone, without anyone noticing what he drove or where he went. The man imagined that he was invisible, hiding in plain sight.

###

The local police knew Carmen Suárez, the young woman who went missing that night. At noon the next day, an El Centro police cruiser was parked next to the side of the deserted highway a couple of miles from the town's center.

Officer Manny Ruiz looked at the body of his second cousin, Carmen Suárez, a nineteen-year-old with a six-week old baby She lived with her seventy-year-old grandmother. He knew she had turned to prostitution at fourteen when her mother died. He spoke into his two-way radio. 'This is Ruiz, I'm about four miles outside of town on Highway 86. I just found Carmen's body. She was stabbed in her side. She was dumped in the dirt like trash, with no identification or money.'

'Okay, Manny,' said the dispatcher. 'Stay there. An ambulance is on the way and a few more officers to help with the crime scene.'

Manny looked away and cried for himself. And for his family's loss.

This was the sixth crime of this type in Imperial County since 1933. All were the same mode of operation, and no arrests had been made during this period. No person came forward who had seen the old pickup truck or the man who had committed the crime.

The man who killed her was most likely not from the Imperial Valley. The killing of prostitutes was rare here.

The news of the death was front page news in the local newspaper the next day, but barely made a ripple beyond that. Carmen Suárez became a forgotten human being in the land of plenty.

The El Centro Police didn't have a clue who committed this crime. There were no witnesses, no leads, no motive, just another death in the hot desert. A state-wide notification was sent out by the California Department of Justice a week later. The state police began looking for similar crimes.

CHAPTER 25

The first place I visited to find Barton Haskel's killer was the Cowboy Bar & Grill. Barton had retired from the sheriff's department in 1950, after a twenty-year run as a good deputy. He never married or had any kids. He dated local women but it never got to the serious stage. The word in town, and to his few friends, was that he had bought into the Cowboy Bar & Grill just before his retirement, using whatever money he had squirrelled away as a deputy. No one really asked Barton about his private life; he never talked about it with anyone, not me, or even Merrill.

Juan was in the kitchen when I arrived, and we went out back to talk, while he had a cigarillo.

'I need to ask a few questions about Barton Haskel.'

'Okay, Señor Jim. Ask away,' Juan said, his eyes, already red, tearing up.

'Did Barton have any problems here at the Bar?'

'Si, Señor Jim, Señor Barton had some people who didn't like him and some he didn't like.'

'Who, Juan? I need the names of Barton's enemies, inside and outside the bar.'

'They weren't enemies,' Juan said, 'just rowdies, but the last night I saw Señor Barton, the night I drove you home, there was a fight with two cowboys, after we left. Mi esposa, Carmen, told me after I got home, those boys were drunk and causing trouble. Señor Barton took them outside and the bigger one threatened that he would return and get even with Señor Barton.'

'Who were they, Juan?'

'I think cowboys who work out at the Circle W, Oakley and Mason.'

I would have a talk with them. 'Anyone else, Juan?'

'There was Señor John Gates. Señor Barton beat him up and fired him back in July.'

'John Gates, huh? Who's he?'

Juan looked uncomfortable. 'He come to town when you are…uh…'

'I get it, when I was drinking. What was the fight about?' 'Probably nothing much. Señor Barton and Señor John

fought a lot while they both worked here. I heard that Señor John is working in Banning at The Red Caboose Bar & Grill.'

I had a sudden thought. I knew Barton was part co-owner of the bar. 'Who's the other owner of this bar, Juan? Who's Barton's silent partner?'

'I don't know his name. Señor Barton said he's a Hollywood producer who comes up to the bar from Los Angeles every three or four months. He was here that last night with Señor Barton.'

That was interesting news. 'Juan, think. This movie producer, you must have heard his name.'

'I no se, Señor Jim.' 'What does he look like?' 'A gringo, Señor Jim.'

'How old? Tall or short? Weight? Any tattoos or marks?' 'About Señor Barton's height and weight. Older, with dark

black eyes. No tattoos.' Juan looked off and then remembered. 'He has a round mark on his neck, on the right side, darker than his skin.'

'A dark birthmark? How big? The size of a quarter? A fifty-cent piece?'

'Bigger. Silver dollar size.'

I could find out who this was, from town tax records. 'Thanks, Juan. This information is a big help.'

'De nada, Señor Jim.' Juan smiled, glad that he could help.

I smiled at my old friend. I knew Juan always wanted to please anyone he met. That's just the kind of man he was.

'One more question. Was Barton seeing anyone from town that you know of?'

'Si. There was Señorita Edith, from the sheriff's office, but they stop seeing each other years ago.'

Everyone knew about that. 'What about recently?' Juan paused to think.

I waited for him to continue, letting the man think about what he wanted to tell me without any interruptions. No sense rushing a story and run the risk of Juan becoming confused, or losing his train of thought.

'Señora Lottie Pilgrim, from town, but that was no big deal. Señorita Lara Aartz who lives in San Diego. Señor Barton was muy en el amor, you say in Americano, very in love? Señor Barton went on many trips to San Diego and always came back happy. Señorita came to the bar a couple of times and Señor Barton couldn't talk. He was what you called tongue...'

'Tied, Juan?'

Si, Señor Jim, he was.'

Juan needed to go back to work and I didn't have any more questions. I wanted to follow up on the information Juan gave me. I was on my way out the door, not even tempted to have a drink, when I saw two men who looked out of place in Lone Pine.

'Hello, gentlemen, I'm Sheriff Jim Cobb of Inyo County. Are you the two men who found the dead man, Barton Haskel, out in the Movie Flats?'

'Yes, Sheriff. Let me introduce my assistant, Reginald Martinson, and I'm Chauncey Donaldson, the location director from Trident Pictures. We are here scouting outdoor location settings to shoot Trident's science fiction film, *Solar Expedition*, set to begin shooting in February and staring Sir Laurence Olivier.'

'Glad to hear that, Mr. Donaldson. The county can always use movie work. I have a question—how did you find the car?' 'Reggie and I were driving around the flats and we came across a motor car parked about one hundred fifty meters off the road.'

I was stumped by the distance and asked, 'What is that in feet?'

'Oh, I'm sorry, Sheriff, that would be...' 'Sir, I think that is about five hundred feet.'

'Thank you, Reggie. Yes, Sheriff. Five hundred feet,' Donaldson said. 'The vehicle was pointed away from the road, alone, isolated. As if the poor bugger inside didn't want to be found right off.'

'You went up to the car, right? Sorry to put you through this, but what exactly did you see?'

'Not at all. He was slumped over the steering wheel with his eyes wide open, looking out the side window.'

'I never saw a dead person before,' Reggie squeaked out.

I sensed that our discussion was over. 'Thank you, gentlemen. You've helped my investigation a good deal.'

'Of course, Sheriff, glad to help. Anytime.'

I left the bar more determined to solve the case and to not have another drink until I succeeded.

The same questions kept going through my mind. A lot of people had the means and the opportunity to kill Barton Haskel. But who had motive?

I needed to talk with Lottie Pilgrim, John Gates, and Lara Aartz. I also needed to find the movie producer who was the secretive co-owner of the Cowboy Bar & Grill.

I wanted to get into the head of Barton Haskel, an area I wasn't aware of when he was working at the sheriff's department. The first person on my list was Edith Pearson from my own office.

Did Edith have any answers?

CHAPTER 26

Archie Reid arrived in Lone Pine the day before Jim Cobb spoke with Juan out behind the kitchen of the Cowboy Bar & Grill. He had driven his 1947 Pontiac Streamliner sedan coupe, Burbank green upper and Asbury green lower, south from Modesto, past Bakersfield, and through the Tehachapi Gap, then north past Indian Wells into Inyo County.

Archie drove to the Trailways Bus Station in town to wait for his army buddy, Reinhard, from Chicago. Archie was thinking about Gretchen while he waited. By now, she would be at work in the wine packaging area. He had read her note a thousand times since he found it after stopping for gas in Bakersfield. Archie knew that there was life after his trip to Lone Pine, if he didn't have to go to prison.

Reinhard had caught a DC-7 out of Midway Airport to Los Angeles, an hour after the two men had talked the day before. The bus ride from LA brought the friends together before noon. The crisp, clear autumn weather was an unexpected change from Indian summer in Chicago and the dry heat of Modesto.

Archie and Reinhard were happy to see each other, the first time since leaving the army. The two army buddies had stayed in touch since the end of the war. Archie exited his car and rushed up to Reinhard, instant recognition in both men's eyes. Reinhard dropped his bag on the sidewalk. Each man shook hands firmly while holding the other's opposite upper arm. They stood there, smiling, holding on to each other, not wanting the moment to end, imaging this a dream if they released their handshake.

'Archie, it's you, almost twelve years and you haven't changed one bit. Still the country boy with a mile-wide grin.'

'Yes, Renne, the country boy came to meet his city slicker friend. How's everything in Chicago?'

'Good, the delicatessen is doing well, and I met a girl, Sonja.' Reinhard smiled. 'She came over after the war from the same little village in Germany my parents were originally from.'

'That's swell. Gretchen's going to have my baby next spring.'

'Good, Archie. Congratulations.'

Nothing else needed to be said. Reinhard knew about the rift between Archie and his family, especially from Silas, Archie's father.

Archie and Reinhard drove to the Mount Whitney Motel, where Archie already had a room. The two friends needed to discuss their plans. Archie parked the car in front of the motel and pointed across the street.

'We need to talk with Barton Haskel at the Cowboy Bar & Grill,' Archie told his friend 'He and Silas worked together, robbing rich Hollywood people when they worked on movies up here in Lone Pine.'

'You never told me about that. You have to tell that to the sheriff.'

'Not yet,' Archie said. 'First, I want to find out what's going on in town.'

The noontime crowd was picking up inside the Cowboy Bar & Grill. As Jim Cobb departed the Cowboy Bar & Grill, he noticed two men get out of a green Pontiac in front of the Whitney Motel.

CHAPTER 27

Edith Pearson had taken some time off work after learning about Barton's death. I went to her house.

Grady Bennett, the reporter from the *LA Post*, was opening the door as I started to knock. 'Edith is resting.'

I pushed my way into the house and called out. 'Edith, it's Jim. Come out and join me in the kitchen. We need to talk.'

After introductions, Edith and I sat across from each other at the kitchen table. Her new boyfriend, Grady, sat behind her, out of place, but wanting to be in on the discussion.

'Edith, when Barton worked at the Sheriff's office, did he have any friends outside the department? That you knew of?'

She shook her head. Not that I recall. Wait, there was a man he mentioned from time to time, he called him Sailor. I never met him or saw him. Barton said he lived off the map, by himself, out in the woods like a feral dog. Maybe some place out near Death Valley. Or farther east.' Edith sat back in her chair and remembered another tidbit of information she had heard. 'He did say something once that caught my attention. This man called Sailor had a difficult time reading and writing.' I nodded as I wrote this down. 'Did Barton have a silent partner, do you know? Or maybe someone who was the real owner of the Cowboy Bar & Grill?'

'There was one time, about ten months after we started dating. I overheard him talking with some Hollywood type about the bar, but he never told me his name. Barton never talked about the business in front of me ever again.'

'Did you know anything about a man named John Gates?' 'Gates? He worked here in the bar for a couple of months.

When you were…'

'Yeah, I know. So what was the relationship between him and Barton, do you know?'

'Where he came from, or if there was any other history between Barton and Gates, I never heard. I will say one thing, Barton and Gates hated each other. They had a big fight and Barton fired him. He left town the very next day.'

Could this have led to murder? I made mental note.

Not sure if Barton would have told her, I had to ask. 'Did you ever hear about a woman named Lara Aartz?'

A smile came over Edith's face. 'Ah yes, good old Lara Aartz, the woman who came between Barton and me.' She laughed good naturedly. 'Barton met her eight years or so ago at a big Hollywood event in Lone Pine. A guy by the name of Darren Harris set everything up. The father was a retired assistant mucky-muck something or other from Switzerland or some place, I don't really remember.

Edith paused, perhaps remembering Lara and Barton at the Majestic Pictures event. 'I do recall that Harris and Barton were close there. Maybe Darren Harris is the owner of the Cowboy Bar?'

'That's good information, I'll look into it.' I wrote down the name. 'Edith, is there anything else you know about Lara Aartz?'

'Well, I can tell you that Barton met Lara and fell head over heels in love with her. It the major reason Barton and I broke up. Aartz is beautiful, a real stunner with class, and a pedigree. After she arrived in Barton's life, there was no one else.'

'Can I get you a drink, Sheriff?' asked Grady. I figured this was his way to make himself look a part of the conversation.

'No, I don't want one,' I barked at the interloper. 'What were you saying, Edith?'

She grinned at me as she continued. 'Well, apparently Mr. Johannes Van Aartz kept a tight rein on his daughter, but Barton found a way to get close to Lara. He said she was starved for any attention other than that of her father. Like she was out in the wilderness, hungry all the time. Barton always returned to town like a kid in a candy store and everything was free for the taking. He said he was in seventh heaven.'

Edith stopped, remembering how happy Barton had been and that he was dead, sadness washing over her as she reached for a tissue. 'I'm sorry, Edith. I know you two were close.' I felt bad, but

I had a job to do.

'It's okay, Jim.' She took a deep breath and continued. 'He talked about Lara Aartz since he met her. Her mother had died a few months after the end of the war. The family never went back to Europe. After the mother died, the father and daughter moved to San Diego, when Barton met Lara. Barton insisted that Lara was too good for Lone Pine. The last time Barton mentioned her name to me, he said once the father was out of the picture, he was headed for San Diego, never looking back.'

Surprised, I asked, 'Did he say when this was going to happen?'

'No, he didn't. And after Gates was run out of town, any talk about leaving for San Diego seemed to be put on hold.'

After what Edith told me, I realized I needed to talk to Lara Aartz, her father, and John Gates.

There was one local person I needed to know about. 'What was Barton's relationship with Lottie Pilgrim?'

Edith laughed out loud. 'Lottie Pilgrim was Barton's local good time girl before me. She claimed Barton promised to marry her, on many occasions, but Lottie's not that big on the truth, so I doubt it. Rumor was her brother-in-law Silas was sleeping with her since she moved into his family's ranch back in 1944. Sadly, Lottie was the butt of many a joke around the Cowboy Bar & Grill.'

All this information ran around in my head, not making much sense. As I left Edith's house, I caught Grady Bennett watching me. There was something about the newspaper man I just didn't like. I was sure he was no good for Edith.

I knew Edith had nothing to do with Barton's murder, but the other people Edith told me about gave me a good list of possible suspects. Now I needed to get to work and whittle the list down to the killer. But three of the people I wanted to talk with were out of town.

Lottie Pilgrim was a local person with an involved connection to Barton. She had taken care of my daughter for a few years, as a nanny, while Harriet acted out her role as mistress of the house.

I remembered Lottie as a quiet, reserved woman who never said or did anything on her own. She always waited for direction from a person in charge. I hoped what Edith had said was not true. How did she get mixed up with Barton?

And what was Silas Reid's position with Barton?

CHAPTER 28

After my talk with Edith, I drove over to Barton's house to have a look around. We had worked together after the war until Barton retired in 1950. He was the next best thing I had to an older brother who protected me from any harm. I looked back on all the years Barton and I were together, and I could count on one hand how much he talked about his life before coming to Inyo County. He did mention growing up in Mendota, in Fresno County. There was a younger brother, Russell, who died at the Battle of Cape Esperance at Guadalcanal. His mother passed away after hearing about the death of her youngest son. The shock of it killed her.

Knowing more about Barton was a mystery, he was closed mouth, and didn't offer any information about the women he dated, the Cowboy Bar & Grill, or who else he associated with outside the Department. The man was a mystery he created, whether to keep me in the dark or to protect our relationship, I will never know.

He could well have had a hide-y-hole someplace, a place where he kept all his secrets. My question was, if he did, where was it? Did Edith know anything about a secret location? I doubted it, but you never know. Was there anyone else in town who knew anything about Barton Haskel that Edith and I didn't?

I searched through Barton's house without the necessity of a warrant, Barton was dead and I'm the sheriff. From top to bottom, I looked in each room, but there were no hidden spaces or secret rooms to be found. Nothing out of the ordinary. Everything was what you would expect. Even the papers and bills on the desk were all routine. There was nothing about a co-owner for the Cowboy Bar & Grill. One thing it did not look like was a man preparing to kill himself. It was more like he was living his daily life.

The only item of interest I found was a family picture album in a drawer of a nightstand next to the bed. It seemed out of character for Barton. Looking through the album told me the story about Barton Haskel's family, from Mendota, up in Fresno County. His parents had died, and the only other person was a younger brother named Russell, who was fifteen years younger than Barton. The yellowed newspaper clipping said he'd died as a twenty-year-old Marine at the Battle of Cape Esperance on October 11, 1942, on the northwest coast of Guadalcanal. Exactly what Barton had told me.

There was one family picture of Barton, young Russell, and another man, maybe a year or two older than Barton. In the picture, Russell looked like he was no more than ten or eleven, meaning Barton would have been about twenty-five.

Another picture was of a very good-looking woman, possibly mid-twenties. She was standing in front of the Hotel del Coronado, the red roofed, white wooden structure, a landmark on Coronado Island, across the bay from San Diego. I came to the conclusion that this was a picture of Lara Aartz. The clothes and hairstyle made it appear to have been taken in the late '40s. Barton must have taken the picture while on one of his trips to see her. There was no other information about the mysterious Ms. Aartz.

I took the album.

CHAPTER 29

Archie and Reinhard went into the Cowboy Bar & Grill looking for Barton Haskel and saw Juan behind the bar. Juan remembered Archie from before the war, asked him how he ws doing and told him that Barton was dead.

The news of Barton's death stopped Archie in his tracks. The idea that Silas could have killed Barton passed through his mind. 'When did it happen?'

'A few days ago,' Juan said.

Archie and Reinhard went to sit in a booth. The jukebox was playing 'The Cattle Call' by Eddy Arnold.

The waitress came over. 'What can I get you two for lunch?'

The two men answered at the same time. 'Burger and fries.' The waitress laughed along with them.

'Anything to drink?'

'Root beer,' they both said simultaneously.

'Do you two always say the same thing together?' she asked, smiling.

'We do kind of finish each other's sentences. It comes from being friends a long time,' said Reinhard.

The waitress left to get their order.

While they waited for their burgers, Reinhard leaned forward and lowered his voice. 'Archie, are you thinking your father could have killed Barton?'

'It's a possibility. But why would you kill your robbery partner?'

'Maybe we need to find your father and ask him.'

Neither spoke as the waitress brought the burgers. She put a place setting and rolled up napkins next to their plates.

The men dug into their meals after each put ketchup on their burgers and a pool next to their fries for dipping.

The waitress came back with their drinks and set them down. 'Anything else?'

'We just heard that Barton Haskel died. Do you know what happened?'

'Rumor has it he killed himself out in the Movie Flats area.' 'Killed himself?' Archie said, surprised.

'Did you fellas know Mr. Haskel?'

'I knew him a long time ago,' Archie answered.

Archie and Reinhard finished their meal and drove over to Barton Haskel's home and parked across the street. They saw the sheriff just leaving the house, holding something under his arm. Jim got in his patrol car and drove off.

'Let's take a look around,' Reinhard suggested. They went to the back and entered the little bungalow.

A few minutes later, they left with a box Archie knew was in a hidden space behind loose stones in the fireplace. When he was very young, Archie had once watched Silas go to the secret hiding place. They had gone to Barton's to pick up some money Silas was owed. Archie doubted his father would remember taking him there, or that he had seen the secret space.

Instead of talking with each other out in the open, the two robbers had set up a plan to pass information by using the secret hiding place in Barton's house. All Silas needed was to see how Barton parked his truck outside the house. If the truck was across the street, then Silas knew there was a message for him tucked into the hiding place. He only needed to return once the truck was gone.

In their room at the motel, Archie and Reinhard were going through the items in the box. A ledger told the story of all the robberies Barton and Silas had performed on the Hollywood people, what was taken, and how much money everything was worth.

'All those years my mother and I went hungry while he had stolen money in his pocket,' growled Archie. 'Look at this. Wallace Berry, Tom Mix, Joel McCrea. Jeez, even Alan Ladd.'

Archie continued to read, 'Jewelry was stolen from Yvonne De Carlo, Ida Lupino, Terry Moore, and, huh, Rita Hayworth?'

All the items, earring, watches, and bracelets were pawned by Darren Harris on visits to Chicago, New York, and New Orleans. The profits added up in the thousands over twenty-five years. The ledger gave all the dates and the movies each actor was working in.

'Look here.' Reinhard showed Archie a wrinkled papers he'd found. 'It says that Barton Haskel investigated all the crimes, but only recovered items from a few of the robberies, and returned them to the owners. 'Are you ready to go to the sheriff now?'

'Not yet, Reinhard. First, we need to find my father. Ask him about the Hanging Murder.'

'He hasn't seen you in a long time, Archie. What do you think he'll do once he lays eyes on you again?'

'He'll probably want to kill me. I know my father and he'll keep a hate grudge for as long as it takes to make good on it.'

'Well, then…' Reinhard was determined that would not happen. 'I think we need to get some guns, to make sure the fucker doesn't succeed.'

'You're absolutely right, and I know just where to go.'

CHAPTER 30

onday morning, when I entered the sheriff's office, Merrill was leaning over, talking with Marlene, whose desk was off to the side from the desk sergeant's.

My father and Marlene had had a relationship when she started working in the office in 1921. Their affair had been off and on until Conchita came to town and started to work for my mother.

Marlene was looking into Merrill's eyes as if they contained all the wisdom of the world. They were acting like love-sick teenagers. Their display was demeaning, only these two didn't care one bit what anyone else thought.

Marlene had turned fifty-three last month. Single, after a brief marriage in early 1943, when her husband was killed in the war. She was attractive, comely, is how I would describe her. She had deep blue eyes and even features. According to Red, her weight was still the same as when she first started working at the sheriff's office. A very nice-looking woman.

Life goes around and around. Some people sit off to the side, never taking the ride. Marlene never took the ride. She watched, critiqued others, made derisive comments if the person wasn't just like her, and only thought of what was best for herself. My only wish for Marlene was for her to follow her dreams with a cowboy, someone other than my father.

I called out, 'Dad, where's Red?'

Merrill, jolted from his conversation with Marlene, stood up. 'He went to the break area to get some coffee, son.'

I snarled an order. 'Go get him and meet me in the conference room.'

Merrill, a smile on his face, strode off like a junior officer following a command, like he was proud of me for saying it and glad to get away from her.

I was in the conference room, standing in front of the chalk board, writing, when Red and Merrill came in and sat down.

I wrote on the board: Barton Haskel Murder Case. I continued writing, my back to them:

Circle W Hands…Oakley or Mason

'Red, we need to send a couple of deputies out to the Circle W and bring in the two drunken yahoos who got in a fight at the Cowboy Bar & Grill the last night Barton was seen alive.'

Red asked, 'What's the story, Jim?'

'I learned from Juan that Barton ran those two cowboys out of the bar just after midnight. One of them, a fellow named Oakley, threatened Barton before they left.'

'I'll get somebody right on it,' said Red, as he left to find a deputy.

I continued writing on the board:

A man named Sailor—someone who can't read or write. 'Know him, Dad?'

Merrill shook his head. I added to my list: John Gates

Darren Harris Lottie Pilgrim, Lara Aartz Ambassador Aartz

I finished after writing:

Where's Barton's hunting cabin, if he had one?

Red returned just then. 'Deputy Roth is on his way out to the Circle W. I called the ramrod, to round up all his hands who were in town that night.'

'Good. I have some questions to put to you both.' 'Okay, Jim, shoot,' Merrill responded.

I stood in front of the board and pointed. 'First, have either of you ever heard of someone Barton Haskel may have known called Sailor? This would possibly have been someone who couldn't read or write. Edith told me Barton mentioned this Sailor fellow a couple of times but never elaborated about his identity.'

'You would know that better than I would, Jim, I never hung around Barton in the off hours when he worked in the department,' said Merrill.

Red spoke up. 'There were twelve or more years' difference in our ages when Haskel was on the force. We didn't spend much time together outside of work. Barton wasn't a real buddy that you hung around with. And I don't recall ever hearing him talk about anyone named Sailor.'

'Did you ever hear of a secret hiding place Barton had, or might have gone to, possibly a hunting cabin?'

'No, Jim,' said Merrill. 'Whenever the department went elk hunting, Barton was the first to opt out and stay behind here at the office.'

'I never heard Barton talk about a hunting or fishing cabin, or any-place away from town,' Red added.

'What do you each know about John Gates and the relationship between him and Barton?'

'Gates came to town a few months ago, after your wife's accident, actually, Jim, and he started running the Cowboy. He had an old war injury, one of his legs. He only worked behind the bar. He and Barton had it out and Gates left town right after the brawl.'

Left unsaid was that all this happened while I was drinking myself into oblivion.

'I think there was bad blood between the two. I don't think Gates liked being bossed around and Barton owned the bar,' Red offered.

'Barton might not have owned the bar.' That got their attention. 'Some guy by the name of Darren Harris may be the real owner. Ever heard of him?'

'I never heard of another owner of the Cowboy,' Red said. 'Barton did do some side work when the picture people were in town, even back when he worked for the department. He was fascinated by what all those Hollywood types had—money, flashy women, and fast cars.'

'Dad?'

'Never heard of a Hollywood producer named Darren Harris,' Merrill said.

Looking at my list on the board, I said, 'What was the relationship between Barton and Lottie?'

'I knew from the beginning about Lottie,' Red said with a faraway look. 'She's a good woman, but Barton didn't treat her right. I even had thoughts about meeting with her on my own terms, but never got up the grit to do it. Sometimes I wish I had.'

'You should have,' I said. 'You still can. I know Lottie well. She worked for Harriet and me as a nanny for Kendall until she started school. She was a widow with a little son named Woody back then and she had moved here from Oklahoma to live with her sister, Minerva, and Silas. They're her only living relatives.' 'She arrived in town in '44.' Merrill added. 'A rumor went around town that Silas was sleeping with both sisters.'

The room went silent before Merrill spoke again. 'Silas has always been a sneaky, weasel-like fellow who only works odd jobs. He did run a still for a few years after he first arrived.'

'I never did like Silas,' Red admitted. 'He never looks you in the eye.'

Merrill said, 'Silas Reid is a fellow with no friends, the complete loner. I never understood why Minerva stayed with him. They had a boy, I think named Archie, a polite kid, always please and thank you. He went off to war but never came back. Must have been a war casualty.'

'I remember Archie,' I said. 'About ten years younger than me. Rail thin kid, with hollow, sunken eyes. Quiet, he didn't say much, he looked scared of his own shadow.'

'Like he was being beat at home by a mean father,' Red said in a low voice, as if he knew firsthand about mean fathers.

Each one of us had known about men who were just plain mean, never a good word coming out of their mouths. Tough as he was, my dad was never one of those men. I pointed to next name on the board. 'Does the name Lara Aartz mean anything?'

Red replied, 'Never heard of her.'

My father's silence was answer enough.

'She lives down in San Diego. He had a big time crush on her.

He went down there every other weekend or so for years.' They both shook their heads.

The meeting was over. I slapped my hands together to knock any chalk dust off.

'What's next, Jim?' my dad asked. I knew he was gently pushing me a little.

'I need to have a talk with this fellow Darren Harris, find out if he is the owner of the Cowboy Bar. Then I'm driving down to Banning to see John Gates.'

'Good,' Merrill nodded.

'I'm getting Sheriff Deis in Fresno County to find out about Barton's life in Mendota, where he grew up. I don't know what I'm doing with this Lara Aartz woman. She shouldn't be hard to find.'

I decided to leave the names on the chalk board. I would write under each name what I found out after interviewing them.

Merrill left the office in search of a cup of coffee, but he detoured on his way when Marlene waved him over for another private conversation.

I watched my father slide up to Marlene. I realized that Merrill's sole purpose in life was directed by his prick. This fact never ceased to amaze me. I shook my head at the thought of Merrill with any women other than my mother. The idea left a sour taste in my mouth.

Red glared at Merrill as he sat with one hip on Marlene's desk. 'I'm glad your back on the job, Jim. We, all of us in the department, need you back at work.'

The department needed my presence? I needed the job more. This job was all I had. It gave me a reason for living, a purpose to wake up every morning, and something I was damn good at. Better than my father.

I thought about Conchita. She was the one person, along with my mother, who always wanted me to triumph in life.

I put my hat on and said to Red, 'I'm think I'm going to go have a talk with Lottie Pilgrim.'

CHAPTER 31

Grady looked around Edith's small cottage and felt hemmed in on all sides. The quiet life was not in his future. He wanted all the bright lights he could find. The more the better. Feelings didn't matter. He had to keep his name in the public's eye with his byline. He knew that as long as his articles made it into the newspaper, he was important in the eyes of the money people back in Los Angeles.

Two unexplained deaths were twice the drawing power in his favor. Two location directors stumbling across the body of a retired sheriff's deputy out among familiar movie location settings was a big story in L.A, it didn't matter if it was suicide or murder. It gave the readers a reason to appreciate the crowded urban setting versus the high desert rural location's seemingly false idea of security.

Fear was what Grady sold in his stories. Keep John Q. Public afraid of the dark, his own shadow, and the presumed safety provided by the police. Grady wasn't for or against anything, really, he only wanted his name known so he could make it into the big-time city papers. Papers like the *Washington Post, Chicago Tribune, possibly the Los Angeles Times, or even the cherry on top of the ice cream soda, the New York Times.* Grady dreamed big; if you're going to fantasize, reach for the stars.

The story about Barton Haskel ran the next day in the Los Angeles Post above the fold. A recap of the Hanging Murderer and his exploits of the last twenty-five years, in all its gory details, kept the readership wanting more.

Anyone who said that Grady Bennett had a heart or cared a rat's ass about another human being was sorely mistaken. The very thought was preposterous in the mind of a man who was on his way up. The little people along the way would find their own path after he left town. No one remembered the little people.

He knew a journalist didn't need a pedigree from a fancy university, old boy ties to a fraternity, or granddad's money to ensure success. A real journalist only had to rely on his last story. Momentum was the catch, keep the population wanting the next bit of information, don't give it out all at once. Give a little at a time. Keep the unwashed hordes hungry with their mouths salivating for the next scrap. Keep them guessing who the real killer was. Gossip, and word of mouth fanned the fires of discontent.

Heady thoughts twirled around in Grady's mind, the way champagne bubbles tickled his nose before slyly sneaking up on his psyche, making him drunker then when he was swilling down hard liquor.

The phone rang, jolting the Hollywood reporter out of his reverie.

Grady picked up the phone with high expectations. 'Hell-?' 'Last warning, newspaperman. End these hateful stories about Lone Pine or suffer death at the hands of your own private executioner.'

'Who is this?' Grady demanded. 'Ask Haskel.'

'Who the hell are you?'

The line went dead. Grady shook violently as he held the receiver, looking at it, willing the phone to reveal who his caller was. He was white with hatred. If looks could kill, Grady was willing to cross the line.

How was he going to end the threats? Who was the caller? Grady was scared for his life, but he was even more disconcerted about not reaching his dream as a major newspaper reporter.

Grady knew that in rural Inyo County, to make a phone call, you had to click for the operator, give her the number you wanted to call, and the connection was made. Getting information as to who made the call was next to impossible.

Grady clicked the bar on the phone to get the operator anyway. 'Yes, I received a call a couple of minutes ago, could you tell me who made the call?'

CHAPTER 32

China Lake was a Naval Air Weapons Station at the southern end of Inyo County, where Inyo, Kern, and San Bernardino Counties met. The desolate high desert area next to a military installation was the ideal location to get a handgun from an unlicensed dealer. Archie knew just the right man, Henry Platt. Archie had heard about Platt a couple of months before he'd enlisted in the army. The plan was to get an untraceable weapon and, with Reinhardt's help, kill Silas.

Platt lived in a dilapidated building once used as a hardware store, away from any prying eyes. He was sixty, but looked eighty, and only had a couple of teeth. His few wisps of pasted down hair crossed over his almost bald pate. His clothes were worn and dirty, and his body odor met the two friends at the door. A worm of a man who chiseled out an existence like a scorpion under a rock, always waiting for the next easy prey to come within his grasp.

Platt sold guns. Handguns, rifles, and shotguns to anyone who wanted a weapon without the need of forms, licensing, or government intrusion, no questions asked. Cash was the only form of payment.

Each man procured an M1911 .45 caliber pistol, a semiautomatic. The same gun they had used as paratroopers in the war.

Returning from China Lake early the next morning, the friends didn't want to go to the Cowboy Bar & Grill for breakfast. They drove to the other side of Lone Pine and found the Sunny Side Up Coffee Shop.

They sat at a booth and ordered ham and eggs with coffee. Archie spoke. 'We can set up a meeting with Silas at Barton's house by using the pickup truck.'

'What if your father has already heard about Barton's death? If Silas thinks it's a trap, there's no way he would fall for it. I think we should go to your family and confront Silas. Catch him off guard.'

The idea of seeing his father gave Archie an upset stomach. He had hated Silas since he was a little boy. The fights between Minerva and Silas, the beatings by Silas to keep the boy in line, and the Hanging Murders. It all added up to a nightmare relived in Archie's mind every time the thought of family crept into his subconscious.

In his heart, Archie knew he could never tell his mother about the baby he and Gretchen were going to have next spring. The very thought that his child would see or ever know about Archie's own parents made him feel nauseous and weak.

There was no easy way out of this dilemma. They ate their eggs and had another cup of coffee. The silence made the two men uncomfortable. Reinhard didn't want to push his best friend into a corner. He knew that Archie needed to come to his own conclusion and find his way out of the dark by himself.

After thinking about a confrontation with his parents, Archie looked at his friend and decided on a course of action. 'Let's go have a talk with the sheriff,' he said.

Reinhard smiled with relief when he heard Archie's decision. 'Now you're taking, buddy.' He beckoned the waitress. 'Check, please.'

'Reinhard, before we go, I want to call Gretchen and see how everything is at home.'

'Sure, Archie. I'll wait in the car.' Reinhard replied as they left the coffee shop.

Archie called Gretchen from the pay phone booth outside the coffee shop. She picked up on the second ring.

'Hello? Archie, is that you? Where are you? What's happening?'

'I made a decision. Reinhold and I are going to see the sheriff and tell him the whole story about Silas.'

'I know it's hard, but I believe in you, Archie. You'll do the right thing. I love you, come safely home.'

'Thanks, Gretchen, I love you too. I only want us to be happy together with our baby. I'll call after I talk with the sheriff.'

CHAPTER 33

Before I could drive out to Lottie Pilgrim's house and question her, she came into the sheriff's office.

'Lottie, good to see you again. It's been a while. I was coming out to your place to ask you a few questions.' I held the door to my office open and directed her to a seat.

Lottie sat in a chair in front of my desk.

I never knew Lottie to be a talker. This time around, she became a woman with a mission to tell all she knew in the shortest time possible. She spent the next few minutes talking in rushed sentences about her romantic involvement with Barton. She also told me of her knowledge about Barton and the robberies she said he'd committed over the last twenty-five years.

'You knew about that? And you didn't come forward?' 'Well,' she equivocated, 'I didn't know until the end, the

very end.'

'Where did he hide the loot?'

She shook her head. 'I wish I knew.'

'Do you have any knowledge of a hunting cabin Barton owned? Or used?'

'I heard him talk about a cabin he went up to in the Inyo National Forest, high up in the Sierras.' She took a breath, 'Barton told me the cabin was in rugged country and hard to get to. No real roads, and definitely no personal comforts for a woman. No indoor plumbing and the like. He gave some half-ass directions, inviting me, but I never went up there.'

'I'd like the directions to the cabin, what you remember of them. But first, do you know if Barton had a friend he called Sailor?'

Lottie hesitated. I noticed her actions and kept the information in the back of my mind. She became fidgety in her chair, rubbing her hands together in a nervous manor, not wanting to say another word on the subject. Her eyes darted away from me and searched around my office, trying to find something to latch onto.

'No, Jim, I never heard Barton talk about anyone called that name.'

'Did Barton have a silent partner, from Hollywood, in the bar?'

Relieved to be on more solid ground, she said, 'Yes. Darren Harris. Barton called him his little Hollywood boy.' Lottie smiled and continued. 'Darren wasn't a silent partner, there was no partnership. Darren Harris is the sole owner of the Cowboy Bar & Grill.'

I made a note for myself to find out more about Darren Harris and if this is true.

'What about John Gates?'

'Barton hated him, Gates. He ran him out of town.' Lottie looked even more uncomfortable when she said his name, like there was something she didn't want to tell me. Looking around the office, she said, 'I don't know where he is now.'

I didn't let on that I was aware that Gates was now in Banning, running another tavern. 'Did you ever hear about a relationship Barton had with a woman named Lara Aartz?'

This question stopped Lottie in her tracks. Coming out of her daze, she again looked around my office for something she could use to change the subject. After a minute, she came back to earth. 'Barton mentioned her name once or twice. He would disappear for a few days and when he came back to town, he said he needed time alone. But he never told me where she lived or if he had a relationship with her.' Lottie looked more and more jittery. 'Um, I have to go.'

'Before you go, can you write down the directions to Barton's cabin?' I handed her a pad and a pencil.

She wrote down the sketchy directions to the cabin and gave the paper to me. Then, like a lightning bolt, she jumped up out of the chair. 'Thank you for listening.' She rushed out of the office, faster than fresh butter melting in a hot skillet.

I sat back down at my desk and asked myself why Lottie had really come to the office. Did she have an ulterior motive in implicating

Barton in the robberies? Even though people said they were lovers, she didn't sound like they had a close relationship.

What did Barton Haskel do to you, Lottie? Was it the other woman, Lara Aartz, or was it something else?

CHAPTER 34

Wellton, Arizona was a little spit of a town east of Yuma, near the Mexican border. The old Chevy crawled into town well under the speed limit.

The heat was stifling, and the idea of a siesta sounded good to the man. Low on gas, he stopped his truck at a Texaco Flying A station. A boy, about sixteen or so, ran out from the office and asked, 'How much gas, mister?'

'Fill 'er up, boy.' He left the heat of the sun and entered into the small office.

Looking around, he saw that no one else was inside. He went into the garage area. It was empty, too. His eyes opened wider as he caught sight of a cement hole in the floor. He looked at the hole, grinning from ear to ear. This garage didn't have a new hydraulic mechanical lift, and this was where a car could drive over for work performed from underneath.

The man came outside, drinking a bottle of orange soda. The cold liquid leaked a little from his lips as he finished, and he felt the syrupy sweet drink run down his chin and into his four-day-old stubble.

'Any loose women around here, boy?'

'I don't know any women like that, mister.' 'Got someplace to eat at around here?'

The boy pointed down the road. 'The diner is always closed between two and four in the afternoon, siesta, mister.'

'Boy, could you make me change for a twenty?' 'Yes, sir.'

The truck was filled, the total $1.92, eight gallons at twenty-four cents a gallon. The boy hung up the hose, wiped his hands on a rag from his back pocket, and went into the office.

The man followed and, once inside, shut and locked the door while his back was to the attendant. The boy pulled the handle on the cash register and the cash drawer came out, revealing several metal sections filled with cash, both bills and change.

The boy turned to face the man and took the twenty to make change. He never saw the eight-inch hunting knife as it swung down from above his head and sunk to the hilt in his chest, just above the heart. His lifeless body fell to the floor with a thud.

The man quickly took all the money out of the drawer. He dragged the body into the garage, where he pulled out his knife and pushed the boy's body into the hole in the floor. The man found a greasy rag and wiped off the blade. He threw the dirty rag into the hole, on top of the boy's body, before putting the knife away in the sheathe at his waist.

The man opened the door to his truck and started the old engine up. He thought that he might head toward the border.

The Chevy truck pulled out onto the empty highway as a couple of puffs of black smoke belched from the tail pipe, mixing with the hot exhaust. The man smiled with the new-found cash in his pocket. His last thought was that he wished the diner was open now. Killing always made him hungry.

He drove west through Yuma, over the Colorado River, and across the border to the little hamlet of Los Algodones. Less than 900 people lived in the sleepy village, no more than a few cantinas and one posada, a lodging house.

He decided to stay at the sparse accommodations for a couple of days, sitting outside in the ninety-eight-degree-temperature, drinking cold beer.

The room had an antique radio and that evening he heard the news from Yuma. The owner of the Texaco gas station found the body of the boy, after siesta time on the day he died. The dead boy was the owner's nephew, visiting from Tucson for a few days. The news story went on to say there were no leads to the identity of the murderer. The man smiled when he heard the news.

That night he went out to the town's only real restaurant for a Mexican feast and enjoyed the rest of his night in the arms of a woman named Yolanda, the waiter's younger sister. In the man's mind, everything was right in his world. The only question for him to answer was where to go next. He decided west, back to California.

CHAPTER 35

I was looking at a police bulletin that had come into the office that morning. A young Mexican woman had been stabbed to death and left by the side of the road, down in Imperial County. The information was horrific, but Inyo County had its own murders to deal with, and our killers were a long way from being identified, to say nothing of being apprehended.

The phone rang, the sound startling me in the quiet office. It was Dr. Crawley; he had performed both the autopsies on Barton Haskel and on the most recent Hanging Murder victim. I hoped he had found a connection between them.

'Sheriff, I have some news on the Barton Haskel case. The victim had ingested a significant amount of orange juice mixed with chloral hydrate, pharmacologically named, trichloroacetic acetaldehyde. It is a crystalline compound used medicinally as a sedative and hypnotic.' The doctor paused, waiting for me to respond. He thought I didn't know what he was talking about.

When I didn't say anything, he continued. 'In layman terms, Barton Haskel had a Mickey Finn given to him. A drink disposed to make him drunk or insensible. Bluntly, Sheriff, even without your knowledge about the deceased using his left hand to fire a weapon, this latest information proves that Barton Haskel was drugged with a sedative, making him incapable of shooting himself. The death of Barton Haskel has now been ruled a homicide. I'll send my official report in the next couple of days.'

'Thank you,' I said and hung up.

The less I discussed with the arrogant physician, the better. What I already knew was now official, from the pompous ass coroner in Los Angeles: my friend was murdered.

I had to find out why. Who was the murderer? How was it accomplished?

My day had started with the Hanging Murder case and now the killing of Barton Haskel. I had two cases to solve and no idea if they were related. Any questions I devised didn't lead me to any answers.

What to do? I moved some papers around on my desk, looking for something to fill my time. I started to feel shaky, unsure of my next step and quickly thought of my go to—old reliable.

I had told my dad and Red I was never having another drink, but right now I needed something to take the edge off. I needed a drink to help me think about some answers. I opened my bottom drawer, looking for the bottle of Four Roses.

The drawer was empty. I feverishly searched for my salvation. Where did I put that damn bottle? I was ready to call out to anyone in the office to find out who took my precious crutch I'd used over the last four months, when the phone on my desk rang.

'Hello?' I barked, not realizing I was yelling.

There was silence at first, then a questioning voice. 'Is that you, Jim?'

'Conchita?'

'I don't want to bother you, I only called to see if you were coming back to the ranch for lunch. You need to eat something before you go to the funeral.'

She was right. Barton's funeral was that afternoon.

'I'm preparing some meat to make burritos con carne asada with jalapeño peppers. I was calling to ask if it was okay or if you wanted something else?'

'Yes, Conchita, that's great, thanks. I'm sorry I jumped at you.'

'I know you are busy at work looking for some hombre, muy malos.'

'Sí, Conchita. I need to find some dangerous men, but they will have to wait until after I come home for el almuerzo, lunch. I'll be home in a bit.'

I hung up and thought about my next move.

The conversation with Lottie Pilgrim rolled around in my mind. I concluded that she dictated the questions and answers for her advantage.

Lottie told me a story that she wanted me to hear, a lie with some truths wrapped around the outside.

No one wanted to hear lies, especially a lawman.

I knew from two sources that Lottie Pilgrim had a long-time liaison with Barton Haskel. It was obvious she was nervous about anything to do with John Gates. And she didn't want to talk about Lara Aartz. What was she hiding? Why didn't she tell me the truth? Was she protecting someone? Herself, maybe? I understand her reluctance to speak about Lara Aartz, that was probably a sore spot. The rest of it didn't make sense.

The directions from Lottie for the location for Barton's hunting cabin were fuzzy. I needed to find out the exact location and called up the County Assessor for the information. The Assessor had no record of a shack owned by Barton Haskel, Darren Harris, Lottie Pilgrim, or anyone named Reid.

I went out to the break room for a cup of coffee. I needed the caffeine to settle my nerves before I went home for lunch.

A ride out to the area where Lottie said Barton's hunting cabin was, deserved a try. I was open for anything to lead me to some answers, even the ones I didn't want to find out. I knew the answers were out there someplace, just beyond what I could see clearly.

CHAPTER 36

Archie and Reinhard were sitting in Archie's car, ready to go into the sheriff's office when a woman came out wearing a smart blue dress and matching hat.

Reinhard said, 'Hat's off, that's the best looking fifty-year-old lady I've seen around. Archie, what's the matter? Are you okay?'

'I think that might be my aunt.'

'You think? You don't know her?' Reinhard asked.

Archie shook his head. 'We've never met, she moved into my parent's house in '44 with her son, my cousin Woody. I've never met him, either, but I would bet my last dollar that's my Aunt Lottie.'

'Do you want to go over and talk with her?'

Archie frowned. 'No, I'm not ready to let my mother know I'm in town. Let's see if Jim Cobb comes out.'

Reinhard was getting a little antsy waiting for Archie to make up his mind about who to talk to. He knew from experience, pushing Archie too much for a rushed decision never worked out well, as frustrated as the situation made him feel.

The two didn't need to wait long for Cobb to come out of his office.

The sheriff wasn't rushed. He casually strolled to the brand new 318 cubic inch 8-barrel, 290 horse V-8 Plymouth police pursuit vehicle, got in and drove away.

Archie and Reinhard watched in admiration. 'That sure is one fucking sweet ride for a cop out here in the sticks,' Reinhard said solemnly.

'The bad guys in the black hats ride fast out here.'

CHAPTER 37

Grady was sitting at the kitchen table in Edith's house, a cup of coffee cooling beside him. He was writing a follow-up piece for the newspaper on his portable typewriter. The sun was shining brightly through the two large windows in the breakfast nook. The sun's warmth felt good on the newspaper man's back as he typed.

The phone rang, wrenching him away from his train of thought. He picked up the receiver.

A woman, who refused to tell him her name, said she knew something about Sailor's real identity and gave him information that had no value and made little sense. Then she hung up.

When the phone rang a few minutes later, Grady assumed she was calling back. 'Okay,' he said, 'tell me your name.'

'Bennett, you were told to stop writing articles about Lone Pine,' the new caller stated in a cold-blooded voice.

'Who is this? This is the third time you've called.' Grady tried to reason with the caller. 'I only report the facts. Under the Constitution of the United States there is still freedom of the press.'

'There is no freedom of the press in Lone Pine, Bennett,' the dispassionate caller proclaimed.

Grady's voice rose in indignation. 'What the hell do you mean by that?'

The voice snorted with disdain. 'In Lone Pine, we take care of our own and you ain't one of ours. Here, we live by the three S's, shoot, shovel and shut up.'

Grady held the receiver away from his ear. Never had anyone threatened him about an article before he landed in Lone Pine. As his internal temperature boiled, his anger heightened. He was ready to take on any monster in the wilderness. Grady wanted to rip the coward's face off. 'What's your name, you coward!'

The line was silent. The caller had hung up.

Grady's mouth was dry. His forehead was sweating, and both hands shook. He rubbed the back of his hand across his mouth. Frantically looking around the room, he forced his eyes to find what he needed now more than ever. He went to a side table in the living room and reached for a bottle of Scotch, took the cork top out and drank a healthy pull of the caramel-colored fortification.

He sat in the leather wingback chair next to the table and had a second, longer pull, then a third extra-long swallow before he capped the bottle. Never in his life had he ever experienced this level of anxiety.

Grady had almost enough courage from a Scotch bottle to go out and find the creep putting his professional existence and even his life in jeopardy. Just like the cowboys of the Old West, he'd buy a six-shooter, hunt the varmint down, and reign triumphant before his lady love.

Then the grim reality of life hit Grady squarely in the face. Before he ran out of Edith's house making a fool of himself, or worse, getting killed, Grady came to his senses and had another long swallow of courage, admitting he was beside himself with fear. The unknown caller had almost pushed him over the edge. Another ten minutes passed while Grady's breathing and heart rate returned to normal. Who was making the calls?

Grady wasn't sure what was he going to do.

He had to tell Jim Cobb. That was the answer that would restore his sanity. He needed to speak to the sheriff.

CHAPTER 38

Jim left the sheriff's office and drove home for lunch.

At one-thirty, he and Conchita drove to the Perpetual Light Cemetery at the edge of town.

By two, the funeral ceremony for Barton Haskel was ready to begin. In attendance were the members of the sheriff's department who had known and worked with Barton. A couple of CHP officers who knew him stood at the edge of the group, along with Edith Pearson and Grady Bennett. Retired sheriff Merrill Cobb was present. Conchita was at Jim's side for emotional support. Also, in attendance were the Cowboy Bar & Grill employees, including Juan and his family. Plus the towns-people he had served for so many years.

Not present were Lara Aartz, Lottie Pilgrim, or Darren Harris.

Archie and Reinhard watched the proceedings from their car, parked on a hill about 100 yards away.

The quiet, dignified, somber burial took all of twenty minutes. The minister of the Baptist Church gave the eulogy, Red and Jim each said a few solemn words about the loss of a friend and fellow officer.

The casket was lowered into the ground, and the mourners left in their individual cars. Archie and Reinhard followed as most of the people from the ceremony drove to the Cowboy Bar & Grill. The post-funeral gathering was organized by Juan, his family, and the other employees of the bar. Everyone went inside while Archie and Reinhard parked down the street. They watched and waited outside to see if Silas showed up.

The Cowboy Bar was officially closed, but inside, a long table with a white tablecloth was set out, with a wide array of food platters. The twenty-five or so friends and acquaintances were all holding drinks of some kind as toasts, paying tribute to Barton Haskel's life as a deputy, owner of the bar, and a good friend, were made. Jim held up his glass of soda.

Anyone who bared his soul said kind, if not entirely true, stories of the way Barton lived his life. No one spoke about any robberies, or about Barton's family from Mendota, if there were any, or whether or not he owned the bar.

The mood was light, the drinks flowed freely. No one in the crowd overindulged and Jim stuck to his ginger ale.

Conchita resigned herself to a background position away from Jim and his father. She found herself more comfortable in the kitchen with Juan's family.

CHAPTER 39

Conchita and I returned to the ranch house from the funeral. We had both eaten lunch and then eaten again at the Cowboy Bar and didn't have an appetite for anything else. She put a pot of coffee on the stove as we sat at the kitchen table.

Merrill came in, wiped out from the funeral, and sat with us as we waited for the percolator to finish.

I relayed the interview with Lottie Pilgrim to my father. 'What do you think about the information Lottie proclaims to know about all the robberies?'

Merrill looked me in the eye. 'Her story, to me, is unreliable. She lacks credibility, Jim.'

The coffee was ready, and Conchita poured each of us a cup. We sat around the table and savored the rich aroma and strong taste.

The caffeine kicked in before I finished drinking mine. My reinvigorated thinking forced me to ask more questions of myself:

What was the location of the hunting cabin located in the Inyo National Forest?

Did Barton have any friends or relatives still in Mendota? What information was there about Lara Aartz in San Diego? The final question reminded me to call my old friend, Roger

Huntly, the chief of police in San Diego. I went into the living room to make my call. I hated to bother him if he was busy, but I needed some answers.

'Chief Huntly speaking, how can I help you?'

'Hi, Roger, it's Jim Cobb, up in Inyo County. How have you been?'

'Hi, Jim, it's great to hear from you. I'm fine, been busy with work is all. How about you?' Roger asked.

'I'm okay. I'm calling to ask a few questions, if you have some time.'

Sensing this was important, Roger replied, 'I've got time for you, buddy. What's up, Jim?'

'Roger, do you know anything about a socialite named Lara Aartz? Her father was the assistant ambassador from the Netherlands during the war.'

'Lara Aartz? The name sounds familiar. Could she be related to Johannes Van Aartz, He is a widower who lives in this huge mansion on the ocean in La Jolla.' He thought a moment before continuing. 'I've seen him in photos in the paper with a beautiful young woman. I assumed she was his girlfriend.'

'I think you're describing his daughter.' I cleared my throat, 'I have a murder up here of a retired deputy sheriff, and she was his secret girlfriend.'

'Whoa, no kidding? Who was the retired deputy?' Roger asked.

'Barton Haskel, on the job for twenty years, retired, then ran the Cowboy Bar & Grill until he was found out on the movie flats in his car with a single bullet in his head. The killer made a mistake, assuming Barton was a right-handed shooter.'

'Barton's Haskel's dead?' Roger responded. 'I met Barton at the end of the war. I was sent to Inyo to pick up a prisoner and Barton turned the man over to me and another officer. Seemed like a real nice fellow to have your back.'

Jim said sadly, 'Barton was the man you wanted around anytime. He met the Aartz woman here in Lone Pine at a movie premier. I hear she is a very private woman, never wanting any notoriety.'

'I can go out to the house and ask a few questions, if you like.'

'Thanks, Roger. I appreciate that. I'll check back with you in a couple of days.'

CHAPTER 40

On the surface, Silas Reid was an unassuming man. His five-foot-six height was just less than average. His weight, one hundred fifty-five pounds, seemed puny for the amount of pain he inflicted on others. At fifty-one, he no longer exhibited the picture of youthful unrestricted exuberance to all things reckless or impetuous.

Killing came naturally to Silas. In 1931, he had killed his own father in Oklahoma and thrown the body down an abandoned well. Since then, Silas had had a complete and utter disregard for other human beings.

He came and went as he pleased, never answering to his wife or anyone else. He had no friends, no drinking buddies, no one he told tall tales to around a fire or kitchen table. Silas didn't gamble, or drink excessively. The money he made with Barton was his to do with as he pleased, never giving a thought to what his family needed. No one could disagree, backtalk, or use derisive words in his presence. He was the epitome of My Way or the Highway.

Fear was the only thing Silas instilled in people. He kept his wife, son, young nephew, sister-in-law, and even his partners-in-crime in a state of unpredictability about his state of mind. Everyone was anxious, always unsure of his mood and his hair-trigger anger. They all tiptoed around him, holding their breath. A good day was when he released his rage on someone else.

Silas and Barton Haskel's robbing partnership began in 1932, when Deputy Haskel stopped Silas on a suspicion of drunk driving. Silas was drunk on his own moonshine, which he was delivering to a speakeasy located in Palmdale, some one hundred fifty miles south.

Silas's business of running illegal alcohol to towns out of the deputy's jurisdiction was a financial godsend to Haskel. The moonshine running transitioned to robbery, once the Eighteenth Amendment was repealed on December 5, 1933.

The day after Barton's funeral, Silas returned home from God knows where and within two minutes was demanding a beer. 'Hurry up, woman, I have to go see Haskel.'

'Barton Haskel was found in his car out at Movie Flats,' Minerva said, happy to give him the bad news. 'Dead from a self-inflicted gunshot wound to his head.'

'Woman, you're out of your fucking mind. Haskel never would have shot hisself.'

'Well, that's what the newspaper said.'

Silas sneered, 'You always believe what's written in the daily?'

Minerva paused, afraid of what Silas might do to her after she answered. The dead air was oppressive. 'About this news, yes, I do.'

'Then, woman, you're fucking dumber than I thought.'

Silas had another beer while he ran Minerva's news around in his head.

He left the ranch and drove up to Barton's cabin in the wilds of Inyo National Forest. Once he arrived, he went through the cabin, searching for anything that looked out of place. Assured no one had been there, Silas went to the secret hiding place used for the stolen goods and the money Barton received from the fenced items. The money he found went into his pocket, it was all his now.

The next thing was to get in touch with Darren Harris. Silas reasoned that Harris might know more about Haskel's death than the newspaper reported. Silas knew that Harris lived in Los Angeles. Where exactly was another question. He could find out the location but going down to L.A. was something he shied away from. Los Angeles was too big, too many people.

No, going to find Darren Harris was not going to happen.

He had a better idea. He'd to go to the Cowboy Bar & Grill and have a little talk with the cook. Silas knew he could make Juan do whatever he fucking wanted, or else. Killing a Mexican was nothing to him.

CHAPTER 41

Edith and Grady were sitting in the Cowboy Bar & Grill having a drink before ordering dinner.

'You know, I received a strange phone call today,' Grady told Edith. 'A woman, who refused to tell me her name, she told me something about Sailor's real identity. She said this Sailor was a man who moved out here a long time ago from Oklahoma.'

'Really? You got a call? At my house? And what a weird call. I've never known anyone from Oklahoma but-' Edith stopped abruptly, stiffening, staring at a man who had just waked into the bar. Discretion kept her from pointing him out to Grady. She knew about the threatening phone calls, and if it was Silas, she didn't want Grady shot dead in front of her eyes.

After confirming the news and hearing the mixed reaction of whether people believed it was a suicide or not, Silas demanded, 'Where's the Mexican who works here?'

The barkeeper indicated with his thumb over his shoulder and Silas jogged past the bar and disappeared into the kitchen.

'That's Silas Reid,' Edith finally whispered. Grady glanced toward the bar. 'What's his story?'

'When Barton and I were dating, Silas was always hanging around looking for odd jobs.' Edith shuddered. 'He gives me the willies.' She paused, before adding, 'I asked Barton about him once. He told me Silas was none of my business and not to ask any questions.'

'Sounds like Barton was a real prick.' Grady looked at Edith. 'Maybe Lone Pine is better off without him.'

'No, Barton was sweet and fun most of the time. He only became weird when it came to business here at the Cowboy Bar.'

'Okay, but it sounds like he was hiding something. What do you know, Edith?'

Shaking her head, she said, 'Let's change the subject, Grady.'

'Okay, for now. What do you want to eat?

'I don't want to eat; I want to leave.' She put her drink down hard, trembling hands. 'Let's just get out of here.'

Grady saw how uneasy she was. 'Sure, Edith. Let's go over to the Harmony House instead.'

Grady paid for their drinks, they left the menus on the table and walked out into the night and got into her car with the intention of driving to the Harmony House on the other side of town. Edith sat in the car, staring at the Cowboy Bar & Grill with her hand on Grady's arm. 'Let's wait here, Grady.'

'What for?'

She sat back. 'I want to see where Silas goes.'

Confused, Grady replied, 'I thought you said you were afraid of the man.'

'I did,' Edith was biting her lip. 'I am. But Barton always told me, look your fears square in the face, don't turn away or you'll die quivering in a hole.'

'And he died anyway,' Grady noted. 'How ironic.' But he was willing to wait and see what Silas did.

Inside, Silas found Juan in the kitchen and pushed the frightened cook up against the wall, holding the front of his shirt. 'What happened to Barton Haskel? It better be the truth, or I'll ship your fucking wetback ass back to Mexico in a box.' Juan was breathing hard and tasting Silas's foul breath. 'All

I know is two men found Señor Haskel out at the Movie Flats in his car. The sheriff's office said it was a suicide,' he stuttered.

Silas growled. 'What else, greaseball?'

'There was a note written by Señor Haskel in the front seat next to him. That's all I know.'

'What did the note say?'

'The newspaper man wrote that Señor Haskel was robbing movie people here in Lone Pine.'

'You know this newspaper man?'

'Si, Señor Bennett, he is with Señorita Edith. They are out front waiting to order dinner.'

'Point him out to me.'

The fear in Juan's eyes sent a wave of power over Silas, and he chuckled in the frightened cook's face. Silas knew the little Mexican was about to shit in his pants. He laughed one more time before grabbing Juan by the collar, choking him.

'Wait, Señor Reid,' Juan croaked, 'I just remember, Señor Haskel told me that if anything happens to him, I give you an envelope from the safe.'

'Well, get it, you fucking idiot, and be lickety-split about it.' With trembling hands, Juan turned the dial on the safe, getting it wrong the first couple of tires. The tumblers finally fell into place. Juan retrieved the sealed envelope and handed it

to Silas.

'That's more like it. Remember, greaseball,' Silas threatened, 'when I tell you to do something you better do it quick, or I'll have your ass for supper!'

Silas went out to the bar. A quick look around didn't reveal Edith and Silas, the envelope under his arm.

Grady and Edith scrunched down in the front seat of her car, not be seen, as Silas drove off in the direction of out of town.

'What do you want to do?'

'I don't think we should follow Silas, I've changed my mind. Let's go to the Harmony House after all.'

CHAPTER 42

The Inyo sheriff's department, with the FBI, and the State DOJ, gathered all the evidence from both the recent Hanging Murder and Barton Haskel's death. Conclusions were sparse in both cases, with no real leads.

The Hanging Murders were reviewed in their entirety, starting from the first in 1932 to the present. In each case, victims were never identified, fingerprints were taken but no matches found. They were all white males between twenty and forty years of age, thin, with gaunt faces, and lean in size, weighing between 135 and 175 pounds and from to five-six to five-eleven, muscularly average for their ages. There were no major identifying birthmarks or scars except for the latest victim's jagged scar, under his left eye, and no tattoos or surgical operations. Eye color of the victims varied: two blue, three brown, and one hazel.

The method of death was the same in each case — strangulation by hanging, with breaking the hyoid bone and cervical vertebrae, followed by almost complete exsanguination by a right to left laceration on each man's neck, cut across the right carotid artery, right external jugular vein, larynx to partial transection of left carotid artery. This information conclusively indicated a left-handed killer.

There were no signs of physical or sexual abuse before death, and no hairs or fibers were present on the victim from an unknown source. There was no evidence of any tissue, blood, or a hair under the victims' fingernails. Evidentiary findings concluded; no suspect identified.

The known facts about the murder of Barton Haskel were simple: he was a forty-eight-year-old white male, with blue eyes, six feet tall, and weighing 195 pounds.

A single gunshot wound, with a starburst pattern of splitting skin caused a stellate pattern which traversed the victim's head from right to left. The bullet was identified as a .38 caliber and the weapon was, without a doubt, the victim's own Smith & Wesson. He had been drugged with chloral hydrate, a sedative. The fingerprints taken inside of the victim's car all belonged to the victim. No fibers or extrinsic evidence were found on the victim or inside the car and, to date, there were no suspects.

The State DOJ put a picture of the unknown murdered man, along with photos of all the other men, known as the Hanging Murder victims, on television, and in all the local and statewide newspapers in the hope of getting information. They sent information about the Hanging Murders in Inyo County to all jurisdictions in California, Nevada, and Arizona, and a request for information about any unsolved murders in those states since 1932.

CHAPTER 43

The cowboys from the Circle W came into my office. The ranch ramrod, a seasoned man looking past fifty, just under six feet and two hundred pounds, without an ounce of fat on a weathered body. He wore jeans and a plaid shirt, both well-worn, his boots came up to his knees and his pant legs were tucked inside. His worn, dusty Stetson filled his hands. He ushered the two cowboys in, the ones who were fighting at the Cowboy Bar the last night Barton Haskel was seen alive.

I shook hands with the ramrod. 'Thanks for bringing them. Saved me a trip out there.'

'No problem, Sheriff. I want to clear all this up before it takes time from the work they need to do at the ranch. This here's Oakley, and that's Mason.'

Oakley and Mason were the image of Mutt and Jeff from the Sunday Funnies. Oakley, as Jeff, was tall and thin, six-four, 150 pounds, with pimples on his forehead and not enough hair on his face to shave daily. Mason was Mutt, five-five, and round chested. He was as heavy as Oakley, making him look overweight with thick, stubby hands, and a facial expression like he was itching for a fight. Like their boss, they were both wearing jeans and plaid shirts, all worn down from hard washings. Their cowboy boots showed wear and tear related to their jobs, and each held his worn Stetson.

I looked at these two young cowboys and thought to myself, in a fight between them and Barton, the winner, hands down would always be Barton. With one hand tied behind his back. My first impression, neither of these yahoos killed Barton.

I shook hands with each man. 'Glad to meet you, boys. Thanks for coming in. Please, have a seat.' I indicated the chairs in front of my desk. 'Why don't you tell me what happened at the Cowboy Bar the night you two got into a fight?'

Oakley started. 'We was havin' a good time with a few girls, drinking some beers. We stayed outside in the parking lot after old man Haskel threw us all out.'

Mason jumped in. 'We all went outside to the parking lot where Barton pushed him and me. We both went flying and hit the ground. No reason for him to do that. Jason's hands was cut up, and he told Barton the fight wasn't over.'

'I yelled at him about kickin' us out and pushin' us around,' Oakley admitted. 'I wanted Barton to know he couldn't do that to men like us. That was it, and we went back to the ranch with three other hands,'

'When did you get back to the ranch?' I asked.

The ramrod picked up the story. 'The five hands all arrived back around one in the morning. I was waiting up because I received a phone call from my friend, Raelene Harper. She lives down in Indian Wells. She was warning me there might be trouble, she saw the whole thing at the bar.'

'If I call Raelene, she will corroborate this story?'

'She sure will, Sheriff, no doubt about it,' he said this confidently.

Asking how to spell it, I wrote down her name. 'Well, what have you been doing since the night of the fight?'

'Next morning, these two and the other three men and me, we all rode up near Topaz Lake to look at the possibility of buying some breeding stock at the Marsden Ranch. We spent five days up there and brought four horses back to the ranch. After we returned with the horses, we all worked together until today when we came here.'

Jotting all this down, I said, 'Well, thank you all for coming in and answering my questions.'

The interview was over and after shaking hands with each man, I sent all the Circle W hands home. I knew these two yahoos didn't kill Barton even before I made the calls.

I called up Raelene Harper in Indian Wells, she verified the Circle W Cowboys account of the night in question. Then I called Hank Marsden up at his ranch near Topaz to ask about the details of the sale.

The corroborating information left me feeling assured that both Circle W hands were a dead-end in the investigation. But I was still without a possible suspect.

CHAPTER 44

My next destination was a drive down to Banning to see John Gates at The Red Caboose Bar & Grill. Banning was a city in Riverside County with some eight thousand hearty souls, a switching hub for the Union Pacific Railroad, along the San Gorgonio Pass. The high desert area was about two hundred twenty-five miles south of Lone Pine.

I arrived at The Red Caboose Bar & Grill on Front Street, across from the Union Pacific Railroad Station, around two in the afternoon. The light from the open door as I entered caused some patrons to cover their eyes from the brightness of the afternoon sun. The blue skies and eighty-five-degree temperature made the inside seem cooler than the actual reading.

A man I assumed was Gates was standing behind the bar, giving an icy cold draft beer to a customer. I was aware that walking up to him caused some people to look at me before turning back to their conversations.

'John Gates? Sheriff Jim Cobb from Inyo County. I want to talk to you about the murder of Barton Haskel.'

Gates rubbed the bar with a wet cloth in his attempt to put some distance between my question and his answer. When he stood up and came out from behind the bar, I saw that he had some old injury to this left leg.

'The fucker got himself killed, and it's just what he deserved as far as I'm concerned.'

'Mr. Gates, is there someplace we can talk in private?' 'Sure, we can go in the office.' Gates yelled out, 'Jumbo, come out and work the bar!'

Gates sat behind his desk, and I took a chair in front. Pulling out my notepad, I asked. 'What do you know about Barton Haskel?'

'He was a no-good selfish fucker to the core. He only thought of himself and everyone else around him was nothing to him.'

The information spilled out of Gate's mouth like a broken spigot. I waited for more and I didn't have to wait long.

'I was managing the Cowboy for Mr. Harris, been there a month or so, but Barton wasn't having it. He told Mr. Harris he wanted the bar responsibilities and presto-chango, I'm out on my ass.'

'How did you injure your leg?' My question put Gates on a new track and caused him to become quiet and thoughtful.

'I was in the 4th Infantry Division in the Battle of Hürtgen Forest late in November '44. Worse place in hell. The weather, the densest forest in the world, incompetent command, and the Krauts with nothing to lose, kept fighting. You in the war?'

'England,' I said.

He reflected on the war and what happened. 'It was just after what should have been sunrise, but the trees in that forest where so close together that the sun never reached the floor. Moss was everywhere. Even the snow had a tough time finding the ground. I was always cold and damp, clear to the bone. Every inch of that impenetrable forest was known to the Germans. They set up numerous bunkers in our area. I was having a cup of Joe at first light when two rounds tore through my upper left leg. I almost bled to death, but the medics were able to stop the bleeding and get me out.'

He paused in his bitter reminiscence for a minute. 'Yeah, after eight operations at four different army hospitals, the Veterans Administration up in Oakland handed me my paperwork and I was put in for partial disability, twenty percent, for life, in 1947. Been kicking around working in bars ever since. The rest is history.'

I returned the subject back to why I was here. 'When did you first meet Barton Haskel?'

'After I came to Lone Pine and started working at the bar,' he replied.

'Did Darren Harris hire you?'

'Yeah, it was Harris who took me on.'

'Was there a fight between you and Barton this past July?' I asked.

Gates curtly nodded his head once. 'Yeah, he beat me up over a comment I made and fired me. I came down here and started working at The Red Caboose a week later.'

'What was the comment?'

'That's none of your goddamn business, Sheriff Cobb.' I moved on. 'What do you know about Darren Harris?'

'He's supposedly a big-time Hollywood movie producer. Maybe more talk than big. He owns the Cowboy. I don't know anything else.'

'Did you know that Barton and someone named Sailor were robbing visiting Hollywood people in Lone Pine?'

Gates paused before answering, 'Yeah, Sailor was Barton's mule. The man did everything for Barton, like a slave. I never knew Sailor's real name or what was the exact connection with Barton, but it went back as early as '32 or '33.'

'Where were you from, before the war?' I suspected the answer.

'Mendota, a little city in Fresno County. My old man worked at the Southern Pacific Railroad storage and switch facility site there.'

I took out the picture of a young Barton Haskel with a man and a boy. 'The boy was Barton's younger brother Russell, he died at Guadalcanal.' Watching Gates's face, I pointed to the other man. 'Is this you, John?'

Gates glanced at the picture. 'I never saw this before in my life. I never met Barton Haskel before I moved to Lone Pine.'

'Was Barton a part owner of the Cowboy Bar?'

He laughed. 'Never. He was just the hired hand, same as me, to oversee the operation at the bar. Barton worked for Darren Harris.' Gates sarcastically added, 'And he wasn't no partner. I gotta get back to work. Don't wanna lose this job.'

'Who owns this bar?'

Gates smiled for the first time. 'Harris.'

I left the bar thinking about what Gates had said.

Barton was originally from Mendota, and the Fresno County sheriff department was looking into any surviving family or friends in the area. Darren Harris was the sole owner of the Cowboy, and he owned The Red Caboose, too. I was sure the picture I'd showed Gates with

Barton and his brother Russell was with John Gates in Mendota when they were young.

I caught Gates watching me from the window near the front door while I was getting into the patrol car. I saw him make a call from the pay phone on the wall by the window. As I drove off, I had the feeling that he was always second in the line of power or command. He took orders and carried things out without question, never asking why to whoever was ordering him.

I made a mental note that I needed to get the information from the Fresno County Sheriff about the lives of Barton and his brother Russell. And find out if Gates was living in Mendota when the other two were there.

What was the real relationship between Gates and Barton Haskel? Where did the bad blood come from?

CHAPTER 45

I arrived back at my office close to seven and saw a message to call my friend Roger, the San Diego police chief. I was reaching for the phone when it rang.

'Hello, this is Sheriff Jim Cobb, how can I help you?' 'Sheriff, this is Grady Bennett. An anonymous source called

me with information concerning the Barton Haskel murder. A woman. She called about a man named Sailor who was from Oklahoma. I tried to get more information, but she hung up without saying another word.'

'Did she say this man killed Barton?'

'She didn't say anything else. What do you do with information like this phoned in to the office?'

The only woman I was aware of who came from Oklahoma was Lottie Pilgrim and I wasn't going to give any information about the case to Grady Bennett. In my mind, it was bad enough the gossip reporter was sleeping with my secretary, I was damn sure not going to let him make hay for the *L A Post* writing about the deaths in my county. I was getting the impression Grady wanted some sort of pat on the back for this news. I wasn't going down that road today.

'I first think about the source, then decide if the information is credible. In this case, I'll ask people in the office and follow up as necessary. Anything else, Grady?'

'No, Sheriff,' Grady replied with a sullen tone.

'Thanks for the information. I'll look into it in the morning.' We each hung up as I thought about what Grady has told me. Merrill and Red knew everyone who'd lived in the county since the 1920s. They would know any and all Oklahoma transplants.

My next call went through to the San Diego Police Department. 'Hi, Roger, I got your message. What's your news? Did you speak with Lara Aartz?'

'Hi, Jim. The news isn't what you're expecting. I went out to the mansion myself and found the front door wide open. I called in more officers before continuing into the house. Johannes Van Aartz was not at the house.'

Roger let the news settle before continuing. 'My officers searched the rest of the house and found Lara in a bedroom, dead from an apparent overdose of sleeping pills. There was a note on the dresser.'

'She's dead?' I couldn't hide my shock. 'What did the note say?'

'She wrote that her father hated Barton Haskel and he would never let her marry him. It went on to say her true love was dead and she did not want to go on.' Roger paused, 'Jim, the article, written by Grady Bennett, detailing the death of Barton Haskel in Inyo County, ran in the local San Diego newspaper. The front page with the article was on the bed next to her body.'

'That sure was a helluva start to your day.'

'Yes, it was. The forensic team was going over the house when the father, Johannes Van Aartz, showed up. He said he was in Palm Springs for the previous three days visiting a friend. He gave us the friend's name and his alibi checked out. The man was overcome with grief after I told him about Lara. I can say that the rest of my day wasn't half as troubling.'

'I bet it wasn't. Is there anything else, Roger?'

'Nothing at this end. The medical examiner is doing the autopsy tomorrow. I'll send a mimeograph copy of the note with all the police reports to your office.'

'Thanks, Roger. Your news opens up another area in the San Diego involvement with my murder case.'

'What are you thinking, Jim?'

'I'm wondering if Lara's death is a real suicide. Could someone else be involved?'

'Spill it out, buddy.'

'Barton was murdered up here, making it look like a suicide. He was given choral hydrate to knock him out before shooting him in his right temple. Barton only shot with his left hand, never his right, meaning the suicide was staged.'

Roger said, 'I'll go over and see the ME tomorrow and ask him to let me know as soon as possible what drugs were in Lara Aartz's body.'

'Right. Thanks, Roger, talk with you soon.'

I hung up and sat at my desk, thinking about the shocking information I'd just received. Someone could have killed them both. But the story gave credence to the woman killing herself after finding out her love was dead.

Barton Haskel's murder was leading to more questions than answers. More people dead, who might be innocent or involved up to their necks.

I let out a yawn and remembered that I hadn't had dinner. I'd forgotten that Conchita would have something good to eat, warm in the oven at home. Yes, home, food, and Conchita waited.

I didn't want to spend any more time tonight on the Haskel case. My neck was stiff, and I was dog tired from the long drive down to Banning and back.

The information John Gates told me wasn't the complete truth. I wrote a note to myself to call Sheriff Deis in Fresno County for any information from Mendota about Barton Haskel.

I still needed to search for Barton's cabin up in the Inyo National Forest.

CHAPTER 46

Conchita had dinner ready for me. She'd prepared my favorite, posole, a Mexican soup made with pork shoulder and hominy. I devoured two delicious bowls. Her eyes lit up with satisfaction as I enjoyed the meal, she'd spent most of her day preparing.

She took away the empty bowl and placed it in the sink, and Merrill came into the kitchen, wanting his dinner. Conchita retrieved a dish out of the oven that was kept warm under foil, the plate contained meatloaf with gravy and mashed potatoes with string beans, a typical meal for my father. He never did cotton up to the exotic flavors and subtle heat Conchita brought from her native country. I relished the change from typical American meals.

Merrill ate his dinner while I told him about my meeting with John Gates and my trip to Banning. The news that alarmed Merrill was that Barton was not a partner in the Cowboy Bar & Grill, from what John Gates relayed. I told my father about Lara Aartz in San Diego, and that shocked him. We talked about all the possibilities that opened up.

Sitting at the table after dinner, I asked, 'Dad, do you know anything about anyone or any families who moved from Oklahoma during your time in office?'

'Yeah, when Oklahoma became a Dust Bowl, we had an influx of them.' Merrill sat back as he continued, 'In the early '30s, a lot of families and individuals from Oklahoma, called Okies, settled in California, looking for work. Many farmers in the Central Valley ran them off, afraid the migrants would steal from the ranchers, or start riots because communists were an unknown radical force at the time. The migrants weren't thieves, just hungry, penniless people. In time, the Okies found their place.'

'The only one I know from Oklahoma is Lottie Pilgrim.' I paused to think. 'When Lottie worked for us here at the ranch, I remember she told me she came out here in '44, moved in with her sister and brother-in-law, Minerva and Silas Reid. The Reid's had a skinny son named Archie and Lottie had a young son named Woody.'

'Lottie came here from Oklahoma, you're right.'

'Did you ever hear of anyone from Oklahoma named Sailor?'

Merrill looked amused. Not too many Oklahomans named Sailor, son.'

Merrill went to his room and Conchita finished cleaning up the kitchen. She looked over her shoulder at me, thinking I wasn't looking at her. Her face said it all—contentment in a place she loved with the person who meant a lot to her.

All I wanted was to tell her how I felt, that I would protect her from now on. Instead I didn't say a word. I looked at her and fantasized about her coming to me across a field, wearing one of my cotton shirts, unbuttoned. We come together, and I feel the heat of her body engulf me as we kiss. She leads me to an area nearby with a blanket on the ground…

'Do you want anything else, Jim?'

I came out of my daydream. 'No, Conchita. I'm good.'

The one woman I wanted more than life itself dried her hands with a dishcloth and retreated to her room. I sat in my chair with my mouth half open, without a sound coming out, as I watched her leave the kitchen. I felt as dumb as a pimple-faced teenager asking the most popular girl at school out to the prom.

I silently admonished myself. I was a thirty-seven-year-old, full-grown man, and the sheriff of Inyo County. Why was I afraid to make my feelings known to her? She'd said she loved me. Once. Did she change her mind? I didn't know what to think anymore. Could I be punch drunk from too much driving around and wanting to find a murderer, or was I lonely, wanting someone in my life who didn't really want me?

I put Conchita out of my mind for the night and decided to find Barton's hunting cabin the next morning. Then I had to find

Darren Harris, somewhere in Hollywood. What could he tell me about Lara Aartz? I also needed to talk with Lottie Pilgrim again. I needed more information about Silas and Minerva Reid. Could Silas be the mystery man named Sailor? Was all this leading to the Hanging Murderer?

CHAPTER 47

Two days after Barton Haskel's funeral, I arrived at my office early, The *LA Post* was on my desk. A byline by Grady Bennett about the Inyo County murders was on page one of the second section. The story detailed all the Hanging Murders and then went into Haskel's death.

My office hadn't released any new information from the LA County coroner's office about the determination of chloral hydrate in the victim's stomach. But the *LA Post* article said, off the record, that the cause of death was suspicious because of the autopsy. How did that information leak out?

My third cup of coffee was cold when Red came into my office, laughing at a joke my father had just been telling him.

They both sat down, waiting for me to explain my early arrival.

'Good morning. I was just reading about Barton's murder.'

Red asked, 'The coroner finally decided the death was a murder?'

'No, the source for the article told Grady Bennett the final determination was on hold.' I let the news story settle in Red's and my father's mind and carried on. 'I heard from the coroner. He confirmed that Barton had ingested chloral hydrate.'

Looking at them, I continued, 'I'm going up to try to find Barton's hunting cabin.'

I drove alone toward the Sierras, there were so many thoughts in my head. The world was changing. America was changing. I knew that eventually Inyo County was going to change, whether it liked it or not. President Truman had integrated the military before I enlisted. The Supreme Court handed down a ruling about ending segregation in schools a couple of years ago. But there still were very few rights for minorities. White people still controlled everything; Mexicans lived as domestics in the mansions in Southern California and on farms in the fertile valleys all over the state.

What would the community have to say behind my back if I became involved with Conchita? Heavy drinking was a way of life for white people, but openly in a relationship with a Mexican was a different dog to hunt. I thought about was the woman I wanted in my life. I needed to explain to her how I hoped she still felt the same way about me. I decided I didn't care what anyone else thought about Conchita and me.

The information Lottie had divulged about the whereabouts of the cabin was hazy at best. The area was large and there were very few good roads, lessening the possibility of my finding the actual cabin.

The day was clear and sunny with some high clouds, way above the limit of Mount Whitney. It was still in the lower eighties in the valley, but in the mountains, it could range around the forties, with the possibility of getting colder, and even snow flurries. I had taken extra clothing—my sheepskin-lined winter jacket, leather gloves, and a thick sheepskin fur lined hat with back, sides, and front flaps. I was ready for any weather.

If I found the cabin, I didn't expect to find anyone in it, with Barton dead.

CHAPTER 48

Atwo-story Spanish Colonial Revival style home sat up in the Hollywood Hills on quiet, tree lined Benedict Canyon Drive. An eight-foot high stucco wall surrounded the property, warding off any visitors. Behind it, a good-sized rectangular pool and a small pool casita were nestled among the lush vegetation behind the main house.

Sitting at a round wrought-iron glass topped table, Darren Harris was reading the *Los Angeles Post*, and enjoying his second cup of coffee at ten in the morning when his world started to fall apart.

Harris, a successful movie producer at Majestic Pictures, was born in New York City, to Polish immigrant parents. In 1918, he had traveled to Los Angeles to make his fortune, there was a name change and deliberate self-induced amnesia of anything about New York City.

He was living the American Dream, but Barton Haskel, his right-hand-man was dead.

By 1931, Darren had already produced a few 'B' movies at the studio when he learned about Lone Pine's movie relationship. Majestic had made several Westerns, and all the outdoor scenes were shot up in and around Lone Pine. He had begun a working relationship with Deputy Barton Haskel way back in '32, a couple of months after he had secretly become the owner of the Cowboy Bar & Grill.

Darren had funneled information to Barton, and Barton passed it on to Silas Reid. They robbed the unsuspecting Hollywood rich while they were in Lone Pine, shooting movies. The partnership worked well for all parties. The money Darren made allowed him to buy his home in the Hollywood Hills, The Cowboy in Lone Pine, The Red Caboose Bar & Grill in Banning, and have a numbered Swiss bank account.

But his best idea had been befriending Barton in the sheriff's department; that made it too easy. Barton, on several occasions, 'found' stolen jewelry and returned it to the unsuspecting victim. Darren didn't care that Barton was dead, as long as it was suicide. He needed to find out all the news he could pry out of the Mexican cook at the Cowboy Bar. After visiting the bar, he would have to find Silas Reid. Keeping a lid on the robberies was paramount. Controlling Silas might prove difficult. Whatever the consequence, Darren Harris was not going to jail, even if he had to eliminate Silas Reid himself.

'Can I get you anything?' It was Manuelita, his housekeeper.

'No, no, I don't want anything right now.'

Darren re-read the article. 'This is a fucking nightmare.' 'What's wrong?'

'Nothing. Only I have to go up to Lone Pine today and take care of a few things at my bar. I'll call the house if I can't get back tonight. I have to call my secretary at the studio.'

Darren abruptly pushed his chair back as he left the patio, and the chair fell backward, crashing onto the Saltillo tiles. He needed to find answers and quickly.

CHAPTER 49

The old Chevy truck drove through Big Bear Lake in San Bernardino County. It was heading toward the little community of Running Springs, scarcely two thousand people in residence, just south of Lake Arrowhead. As he approached, the man saw a small ranch house, a little rundown, and in need of some outside repairs, at the end of a cul-de-sac off the main road.

There were no animals around, not even a dog for company. The man drove up near the front of the house and stopped. He went up to the front door with his hat in his hands and knocked. A woman opened the door, her hair unkempt, her face without makeup, worn from too much sun. Her thin blouse was unbuttoned down to the middle of her chest, her capri pants clinging tightly to her lower body, ending with her calf, and her feet were bare.

'What the hell do you want?' she snarled at the man with the gray-tinged beard.

He smiled. 'I was only asking for some cool water in the heat of the day.'

The woman opened her door and pointed toward the back of the house were the faucet hung over the sink.

The man came to the kitchen and found a spotted glass as he let the water run cool. He drank several glasses full before his thirst was quenched. He placed the glass on the counter, running his dirty cotton sleeve across his mouth to dry off the excess water in his beard.

The woman stood watching him from the entryway to the kitchen.

'Are you done with your drink? I don't have all day,' she growled.

'I'm done, thanks.'

He started to walk back to the front of the house. As he came even with the woman, he put an arm around her and pulled her body next to his. Before he kissed her, he spoke, his hot breath hitting her face.

'Woman, you are the best damn fuck I've ever met in my travels.'

She licked her upper lip with the tip of her pink tongue as she opened her mouth to engulf his.

They went at each other for several minutes, trying to satisfy their hunger.

They separated, each taking a deep gulp of air, as their hearts raced. He picked the woman up in his sinewy arms and carried her to the bedroom. She laughed heartily, knowing what was about to happen. The couple went through this charade every time the man came to town.

The next morning, he rose quietly, not wanting to disturb the woman from sleep. They hadn't stopped until almost daylight. She had a smile on her face from the night before. He was bone tired and thought about taking a shower. He shook his head at the idea, not wanting her to wake up and attack him for more. He left silently, closing the door behind him.

He was driving toward town, about a mile before Running Springs, when he saw a teenage boy walking alone near the side of the road. The man stopped his truck and asked if the boy wanted a ride.

The boy's body was found down the road in a culvert the next day by a man walking his golden retriever.

The man never wanted to talk to the kid, he only knew there was a killing he had to preform, either before or after he indulged himself with a woman.

The many women he had squirrelled away here and there for his delight made his travels even more enjoyable. There truly was a method to the man's madness, at least in his mind. The lives he took were all useless in life's grand scheme. Lost souls who never would have amounted to much anyway.

CHAPTER 50

Darren Harris left his Hollywood Hills home before noon and arrived at Barton Haskel's house in Lone Pine late that afternoon. The five-hour drive was lonely and uneventful.

That evening, Darren was drinking his third Dewar's and soda when Silas Reid strode into the Cowboy Bar & Grill unannounced.

'Well, if it isn't the Hollywood movie producer,' Silas sneered. 'What brings you up here?'

Darren set his drink down. His hand was shaking as he lifted the glass up to his sweaty lip. The mere presence of Silas in the same room put the fear of God into the spineless movie producer. 'I read in the *LA Post* that Barton was found in his car. That is was a suicide.'

Silas snorted. 'Barton didn't put a bullet in his own head. He had too much to live for, especially his woman down in San Diego.'

'Ah, yes, the girlfriend.' Casually, Darren asked, 'Is there any news around town about the killer?'

'Shit, if I knew anything, the sheriff would also know, and the fucking killer would be behind bars.'

'I guess you're right about that, Silas.'

'Damn straight I'm right, Mr. Hollywood.' He leaned in and lowered his voice. 'Hey, I want to know, any more robberies in the pipeline?'

Shaking his head, Darren looked at Silas. 'No, not until next spring. It seems the studios are taking a few months doing only inside work or on the back lot. Now with Barton's death, it will be a good time to hold off on any more robberies anyway.'

'If there's no work, let me ask about running the bar here in Lone Pine.'

'You? What do you know about the management of a bar?' 'Not a god-damn thing.' Silas was grinning. 'But I can scare the shit out of anyone working here.'

Darren shook his head. 'I'm not interested in scared workers.'

'Suit yourself, Hollywood. But don't say I didn't warn you.' Silas turned around and left Darren to finish his drink.

Darren knew, deep down, that Silas Reid's time on earth was limited. The unresolved question was, who was the person to do the job?

CHAPTER 51

The search for Barton's cabin up in the forest was harder than I anticipated.

The trip took about three hours. Once I reached a certain elevation there were only dirt roads, and no numbers or names. The area was densely wooded without a lot of cabins around.

I realized if I wanted a secret hideout, I would want to be out in these woods alone, without any neighbors in sight. After a couple of dead ends, I hoped I was headed in the right direction. Nightfall was a few hours off and I didn't want to end up on the mountain in the dark.

The air was cold, with snow starting to fall, it was late in the day when I came up to an isolated cabin. It was most likely two bedrooms, a large central room with a kitchen area, and a single inside bathroom that was set up to a septic tank. I saw there was also a well for fresh water. From Lottie's information, I was sure this was it. There was no smoke coming from the chimney.

The days were getting shorter, and sunset at the cabin's elevation was earlier than down in the valley once the sun moved past the peak. The beauty and starkness of the terrain were ethereal. Few animals trekked to this elevation.

Barton had found a good spot, nestled near the mountain's face. The thick pine trees created a windbreak, preventing snow falling near the front entrance to get too deep. A sharp drop-off on the side away from the front resulted in a view of any vehicles coming up the empty road from the cabin down the hill, a good half mile away. This was a picture-perfect hideout—alone, desolate, hidden, and enough creature comforts to make a long siege doable, if necessary. Shaking my head, I wondered what secrets were to be found inside.

I estimated the temperature to be in the thirties at this elevation. It had snowed the night before, leaving four to six inches of the fluffy, undisturbed whiteness, which covered the steps to the front door. Drifts of more than two feet filled the area away from the cabin to the drop off section of the yard. There was no sign of a person or an animal walking up to the entrance, and there were no tire tracks in sight, other than from the police cruiser.

I put on my sheepskin lined leather jacket, wool lined leather winter gloves, and my sheepskin hat with the back, sides and front flap before I left the patrol car. I could see the mist my breath made in the air when I stood between the open driver's side door and the seat. My gun was drawn, held in my right hand, and down at my side.

There was no sound, no birds or animals nearby. An eerie, deathly quiet encompassed the solitary cabin on the mountain.

I didn't think I'd find anyone in there, now that Barton was dead.

'Sheriff Cobb! Inyo County!' I cried out. 'Anyone in the cabin, come out with your hands up!'

The only response to my challenge was an uptick of wind blowing snow in swirling patterns off the mountain and down the road.

I stepped around the door of the patrol car and cautiously worked my way toward the front door.

I pulled my jacket collar up with my left hand and held my.

38 in my right hand.

I reached the front door, knocked and called out again. 'This is Sheriff Cobb, Inyo County, anyone inside?'

I pushed the door, unsure of the possibilities behind it.

I raised my gun to waist level, stepped over the threshold and turned my head to the right to look inside.

A single, rifle shot rang out from behind me. The report wasn't too loud, a rifle, maybe a .22. I immediately felt a stabbing pain under the lining of my hat above my ear, to the right side of my head.

I must have fallen face down and landed inside the threshold as I sensed blood oozing from my wound and the smell of iron.

And then everything went black.

CHAPTER 52

The shooter left his hiding place across the road from the cabin. He was slight in build, wore a heavy winter jacket, black felt Stetson, lined leather work gloves, jeans, and worn boots.

There was no movement from the fallen sheriff. The shooter didn't know if he was dead or alive. And he didn't wait around to see.

The wind nudged the door completely open. Darkness enshrouded everything.

Tracks could be seen in the new fallen snow among the small stand of pines across from the cabin. The shooter made his way down the mountain unseen, just inside the tree line, making sure to stay off the snow-covered dirt road.

The air turned colder, with a new weather front blowing in across the Sierras. The Eastern Sierras caused many travelers to underestimate the severity of the weather, since the snowpack was less than what fell on the western side of the peak. Fewer pine trees caused the wind to howl without impediment, reducing the temperature. Jim Cobb lay silently inside the open cabin door, a natural windbreak from the elements. In these circumstances, was anything going to survive the harsh elements? Quiet settled on Barton's cabin.

The patrol car began to make loud ticking sounds. Jim had left the driver's side door wide open, and snow piled up on the front seat. The interior lights were glowing until they went out, leaving the vehicle dark and immovable.

Before the patrol car's battery drained out, there was one unintelligible squawk from the two-way radio, from the sheriff's department in Independence. Even if Jim Cobb was alive and sitting in his car, the sound from Marlene Chambers calling the sheriff was not understandable. The call was routine, and when Marlene didn't get a response, she chalked it up to poor reception and nothing else. She was off duty in ten minutes.

CHAPTER 53

Minerva Reid and Lottie Pilgrim were the only surviving Tanner sisters from Elmwood, Oklahoma, a spit of a town in Beaver County, which occupied the eastern third of the Sooner's panhandle. In the early '30s, the panhandle was a poor agricultural region with a small population, fewer than six people per square mile in an area of eighteen hundred square miles.

Minerva, Silas, and Archie were forced to flee to California with the beginning tide of Okies after Silas killed two sheriff deputies who came looking for his father. He made sure they found his father. Soon, all three bodies rested together at the bottom of a dry well and were never found.

Silas had been a less-than-adequate farmer. He became a maker of moonshine from his own still. The alcohol paid the few bills and kept the family in clothes and food until Silas's father wanted a sixty-forty split with his father getting the sixty. Adding insult to injury, his father drank more moonshine than the business could afford, staying more drunk than sober.

Silas and his father had hated each other for as long as Silas could remember. Killing him in February 1931 gave Silas and his family more money to live.

Silas continued to make and distribute moonshine once the family settled in Inyo County. He crossed paths with Barton Haskel after being stopped for drunk driving that year. The two men formed a quasi-partnership in the bootlegging business until Prohibition's Repeal in '33. They seamlessly slid into a robbery enterprise with Darren Harris, until Barton's dead body showed up at the Movie Flats filming location west of Lone Pine.

Living with Silas had been harsh for Minerva. Drunken physical abuse from Silas came weekly, if not almost daily. She had nowhere to go, and her only pleasure in life was her son, Archie. She doted on him. Minerva's only religion was the protection of her son from his father. She lived day-to-day with Silas's drunkenness and beating. Each morning for mother and son was not a joy to live, but a passing of survival from the previous day, coping with the hell of living with Silas.

Lottie Pilgrim, ten years younger than her sister Minerva, had also lived her own form of hell back in Oklahoma. Life in Oklahoma during the Depression was hard and unbearable most of the time. No money, little food, and no future, at least in the mind of an eighteen-year-old in 1937.

Lottie was the youngest, with no family member to talk to, no one to turn to when the pressures of daily life boxed her in, and no shoulder to cry on when she felt lost.

At the age of nineteen, Lottie met her future spouse, Harlan Pilgrim. He was a big-boned man whose family lived in the town of Beaver, where his father owned the feed store. Lottie thought Harlan was cute and he had money to take her to the picture show. He was her way out of the Tanner family. The couple went out for a year before Lottie relented in the backseat of Harlan's new Chevy to his persistent advances.

It was the sixth or seventh time Harlan and Lottie were on the woolen backseat of his Chevy Sedan that Lottie knew she was pregnant. She told Harlan two months later. The lummox decided to do the right thing and marry his sweetheart. He told everyone that Lottie was the best person he ever met. The nuptials took place at the Justice of the Peace three weeks later. Woody's birth came in the summer of 1940.

Two weeks after Pearl Harbor, Harlan enlisted in the Marine Corps. His military duty took him to the Pacific theater. His death came on the first day of the Battle of Tarawa, on November 20, 1943. Lottie saw the two officers from the Marine Corps as they made their way up her driveway, two days after Christmas, and knew the news she was receiving.

In June of 1944, Lottie and her four-year-old son Woody showed up at Silas and Minerva's house in Inyo County.

On July 4th, Silas went into Lottie's room for the first time. Minerva heard the attack and did nothing, she rolled over on her bed, relieved that Silas wasn't hurting her.

Lottie endured her abuse, along with her sister. The two women became cold in their hearts. The hatred of Silas became the core of their lives, with each woman vowing to the other that they would put Silas in his grave. The Reid house was quiet when Silas went on another trip alone, and the women were happy without him.

Woody was seventeen, just over six feet tall and rail thin, with light hair and hazel eyes. He had no friends, and had dropped out of high school when he was fourteen. He'd been groomed since he was six years old to become a mean-spirited, self-centered, solitary murderer, like his uncle Silas. Woody did everything Silas wanted, or he was beaten with a belt, or worse. There was no moral compass for the young man, and he learned, from his mother and aunt to hate Silas more than life itself.

Woody came and went as he pleased, and his mother never knew what he was doing. He had made his room in the loft of the barn, away from the prying eyes of his mother, aunt, and uncle.

Night came earlier each day on the eastern slope of the Sierras as autumn made its gradual move toward winter. Minerva and Lottie were sitting in the living room watching *The Jack Benny Show* on television when a commercial for Lucky Strikes came on. Minerva lowered the sound. 'How are we going to get the sheriff on Silas's case?' she asked her sister. 'How the hell do I know, Minerva. You know I went to see the sheriff before Barton's funeral and told him about the robberies. Nothing happened.'

'We need him looking at Silas.' Minerva held her chest with both hands as pain flashed through her body. 'I need for Silas to die before me, Lottie. He has to suffer before my life ends.'

'I know what you want, Minerva, and I want the same outcome, just not for the same reason.'

'Yes, Lottie. You want revenge against Silas and Barton for what they made you do. I want justice for all the mean and hateful things he did to me and my boy. He chased Archie out of here and I know I'll never see him again.' The pain came again. Grimacing, Minerva said, 'I want Silas to die. Since that doctor over in Lancaster was correct about my lung cancer, I've wanted Silas in the ground before me. Did the sheriff say anything when you told him about the robberies?'

Lottie thought before answering. 'He did ask me about a man named Sailor.'

'Well, that's the answer.' Minerva smiled. 'Go in and tell Jim Cobb that you talked to me, and I told you about Silas's nickname when we used to live in Oklahoma.'

Woody marched into the room. 'I don't think that you're going to tell the sheriff anything, he's dead. I killed him up at Barton's cabin.'

Shocked, Minerva asked, 'Did your Uncle Silas tell you to kill the sheriff?'

'The attack on Jim Cobb was all my idea. I followed him there. While he was looking in the wrong place, I set up an ambush before he drove up to the front of the cabin.'

Minerva stood up from her chair, slapping her nephew across his face. She wanted to give him a backhand after the first slap.

Woody caught her arm. 'Don't ever do that again or I'll kill you.' He threw her arm down and left the room for his place in the barn.

Lottie was crying. 'What are we going to do now, Minerva?' she asked, wiping her eyes.

'I don't rightly know, but we will think of something.'

The two women sat in their chairs thinking over the catastrophe Woody had brought down upon them.

'The bigger question is, what is Merrill Cobb going to do to the person who killed his son?' asked Minerva.

CHAPTER 54

Merrill came into the kitchen around eight the next morning, looking for some coffee. He'd had dinner with Marlene the night before and then they'd spent several hours at her place. Merrill had crawled out Marlene's bungalow around three in the morning. The cold blackness of the sky showed a million stars as he silently drove back to his ranch for a couple hours of sleep.

Conchita had been up most of the night waiting to hear Jim walk through the back door. He never arrived. She had dark circles under her eyes. Worry and fatigue showed.

'Do you want some coffee, Merrill?'

'Sure do. I need to start the day off alert. I had a long hard night.'

'I heard you come in around three-thirty, making enough noise to wake the dead. I want you to know that Jim didn't come home, and his bed wasn't slept in. I'm worried about him, Merrill.'

'Why didn't you say that from the get-go, woman?' Merrill stormed off to the phone in the living room.

'Get me Red Fowler at the sheriff's office,' Merrill told the operator. He drummed his fingers on the desk, waiting for the connection to go through.

'Red, Jim never came home last night, and he's not drinking.'

Red replied, 'Remember he told us he was going to find Barton Haskel's cabin, up in the Inyo Forest, Merrill?'

'Shit! Come out to the ranch and get me. We need to find my boy, and pronto.'

Merrill had his coffee and a couple of pieces of toast while he waited for Red's arrival.

Conchita took a cup of coffee and retreated to her room. She swallowed some but it tasted bitter and stale. She placed the cup on her nightstand and lay on her bed. She turned over on her stomach to muffle her tears for Jim's safe return.

If he didn't come home safe, she had no life, no reason to live.

When Red knocked on the back door, Merrill was ready to leave. Each man had winter clothing on for the ride up to the Inyo National Forrest.

Conchita heard the patrol car drive away from the ranch.

She said a silent prayer for Jim's return.

CHAPTER 55

Red and Merrill drove up to the Reid ranch house in Red's Chevy Bel Air cruiser. The house was east of Independence in a sparsely populated area, somewhat on its own, away from any others. It was rundown, without paint on the outside wooden boards, a place in need of major repairs. Minerva and Lottie stared out its dirty windows.

Red knocked on the front door. 'Lottie Pilgrim, this is Red Fowler from the sheriff's office. We need to talk with you, open up.'

Lottie opened the door with Minerva standing behind her. The women thought the retired sheriff and the deputy sheriff were there for Silas. Or possibly Woody, who had slept in the barn the night before. They were worried.

'Come in, Red. Please, have a seat in the living room.' Lottie pointed the way. 'What do we owe the pleasure of your visit for?'

Woody had watched the cruiser drive up to the ranch as he hid inside the barn. He wanted to know what the deputy sheriffs were talking about with his mother.

Minerva stood in the doorway of the living room, pale as a ghost, her long-sleeved gingham house dress covering her from neck to ankles.

'We need to know the location of Barton Haskel's hunting cabin,' said Red.

Lottie gave the same generalized location for the cabin that she had given the sheriff.

'Does anyone else in the house know the location?' asked Merrill.

Not meeting his gaze, Lottie replied. 'No one else in the house is aware of the exact location of the cabin.'

Looking around, Merrill asked, 'Where's Silas?'

'He went hunting several days ago. I don't know where at or when he'll return,' said Minerva.

Red turned to Lottie. 'Where's Woody?' She didn't respond.

'He went hunting with his uncle. They left a couple of days ago, two days ago,' Minerva responded.

Red smiled at her. 'Thank you, ladies.' Looking at Merrill, he said. 'I think that's all we need.'

As they went to the car, Merrill read the information Lottie had given on the cabin's location.

'Lottie sure is one accomplished liar about not knowing the location of the cabin.' Merrill paused. 'Or never being there.'

Red snorted, 'She sure is.' Looking around, he continued, 'I don't think Silas or Woody went hunting.'

Merrill glanced back at the house. 'Let's get up to that cabin fast, Jim must have spent the night there.'

Neither man wanted to think about the worst outcome for Jim and stating an opinion about any negative possibility was definitely out of the question.

CHAPTER 56

Archie Reid and his war buddy Reinhard Diefenbach had decided to tell everything to the sheriff. However, they kept missing the sheriff at his office. Archie had all the information about Silas and the Hanging Murders.

Archie knew the right thing to do was tell the sheriff, but he was still, even as a grown man, afraid of Silas. Reinhard understood his friend's dilemma. The idea of doing nothing wasn't a real option.

Archie started to call the sheriff's office three times as he paced around his room at the Mount Whitney Motel but he hung up each time before the operator picked up. He was nervous and jumpy about talking with Jim Cobb. He called Gretchen and told her about his inner conflict with seeing the sheriff and telling him about Silas.

In the end, Archie decided to wait until the next day to see him and to come clean about Silas. The sheriff would decide Archie's fate concerning his complicity in the crimes.

Coming out of the war without a scratch, finding a life-long best friend, and meeting Gretchen Wilder at the Winery in Modesto made his life come into its own. Now he had a life worth living for. Archie was not going to let Silas destroy it, like everything else in Archie's life until he'd enlisted in the army.

Archie remembered all the yelling and hateful things Silas said to him when he was a young boy, not to mention the whippings with a switch. It became worse in 1940 when Silas made Archie watch the fourth hanging murder. Silas went so far as to promise that during the next murder, Archie was going to participate, enabling his only son to carry on the family business. Thankfully, before the next hanging murder took place, Archie had dislocated his right thumb, making it impossible for him to accomplish the murder.

Archie knew he had to do the right thing, for Gretchen and the baby. What would become of him after the sheriff arrested Silas was yet to be seen.

The question in Archie's mind was, is he just as culpable as Silas, since he was at the murders in 1940 and '42. The sheriff had a duty to uphold the law; was arresting Archie part of that duty? The idea of not being with Gretchen and the baby was worse than facing Silas.

CHAPTER 57

After Merrill and Red left the ranch, Conchita wandered around in the house from room to room for hours, not knowing what to do. Now, exhausted, alone, and with emotions rubbed raw, she went to the sheriff's office to see if there was any news about her man. Before she was able to ask Marlene anything, Grady Bennett strode into the office.

Edith saw Grady and rushed to his side. They kissed before he held her away. He called out in a firm voice, 'I have received several calls from an unknown person. The caller wants me to stop writing any more stories about the Hanging Murderer. I informed the caller that there was still a free press in America, and I would never stop writing the truth.'

He stood, his hands on his hips and the pride of arrogance in his stance, waiting for recognition from anyone at the sheriff's office. He looked to Jim's office for reassurance for his stand on free speech. Jim's office was dark.

Marlene got up quietly and slunk away from her desk, not wanting Grady to hear her voice and realize she had made the threatening calls. Her reasoning wasn't so logical but it was not evil—all she wanted was to keep Merrill's name out of the newspaper about all the Hanging Murders he hadn't solved. In her heart she knew Merrill would know she was right for threatening the reporter. She had Merrill's reputation to protect. She would tell her lover all about her good deed once she was living at his ranch and warming his bed.

Static came over the two-way loudspeaker at her desk. Marlene came back into the room and clicked a button in response. 'Sheriff's office, Central One, Come in?'

'This is Red Fowler. We found Jim up at Haskel's cabin and…'

The next sounds were garbled and not understandable. 'Red, Red, say again. I lost your signal,' Marlene requested.

'We found Jim, shot, but alive. Merrill and I are taking him to the hospital.'

Conchita heard the news, same as everyone else. She gasped and became light-headed, starting to fall.

Edith caught her. 'Grady, help me, please.'

After helping Conchita to a seat, handing her a glass of water, and waving fresh air into her face, Edith realized the woman from the Cobb Ranch was now stable. She turned to the room and announced, 'Waiting here is not an option. I'm going to the hospital and see him when he arrives there.'

If Jim died, did that mean Merrill's return to his previous duties or would Red take over until a new election took place?

Each person at the sheriff's office thought the worst but hoped for the best.

CHAPTER 58

The Chevy truck drove through Mojave, a little town fifty miles east of Bakersfield. The town had a population of less than two thousand. The man in the truck knew he was close to Inyo County, around one hundred miles south of his destination. He ate lunch at a small restaurant on the north end of town. Enchiladas, rice, refried beans, and flour tortillas. Two Cervezas finished his meal.

It was getting close to three in the afternoon, the woman who had waited on him was ready to leave the establishment, her workday done. The man rolled a cigarette as he waited in his truck behind the restaurant. The waitress was leaving through the back door when he hit his horn once, and she looked up and saw the truck. She smiled at the man, opened the door, and stepped up and into the passenger's seat.

He drove in silence to her little house off the highway. The room smelled fresh with the blinds closed and the window open a crack. She disappeared into the bedroom in the back of the house while the man went to the kitchen and opened a Corona. He finished the beer in three quick gulps, his anticipation rising.

He took off his shirt as he made his way to the back bedroom. She was under the sheet, waiting. He finished undressing and joined her.

'Come here,' the man demanded. He didn't care for anyone other than his own satisfaction. He told women what they wanted to hear as long as he received what he wanted.

She wanted their time together to last longer, but she was grateful he came by at all. Her only intent was to please him in the hope that he would return. To live in Mojave was harsh, the weather, working conditions, and the lack of a steady man. At least he was there now.

They rolled around on the bed all afternoon as if this was the last time, they would ever be with one another.

The sunset and a cool breeze came through the partially opened window behind the sheer drapery.

The man started to get dressed in silence, but the woman held out her arms and motioned for more. He unbuttoned his shirt again and this time stayed the night. He didn't want to go out on the road tonight. The woman was warm and tender. There was no conversation.

The short interlude was pleasurable for each party. The man knew that this woman wanted more than he was willing to give. He hoped that her wants didn't end their time together. If so, he would have no other choice but to kill her. Keeping a woman, any woman, at arm's length was the maxim, and how the man lived. He never wanted kids, a home, or domesticity. The thought of staying in one place, neighbors, pets, or the possibility of in-laws, was not in the man's cellular makeup.

He was not the kind of man to answer questions from another person, let alone from a woman, no matter how good she was. Live for today, don't think about tomorrow, and never remember yesterday.

Since starting his mandate to kill as he pleased, some eighteen years had passed—a good run—but the man was a long way from being finished. He knew no one paid any attention to an old truck and a dishevel man driving through town. He was neither tall or short, thin or fat, not old or young, just a common person who blended into the background like the scenery in a movie. The viewer knew the scenery was in the picture but was not able to recall the man in the Chevy truck, the background that no one remembered in a film.

This was just the way the man wanted to go through life, unremembered.

CHAPTER 59

Conchita, Edith, and Grady arrived at the hospital, waiting for Merrill and Red to arrive with the injured Jim Cobb. The three stood in the emergency room waiting area, worried.

Edith whispered into Grady's ear, 'What are we going to do if Jim dies?'

'I don't know?' They held each other and pulled apart as Grady asked, 'Will Red take over as sheriff?'

'I don't know,' Edith answered, then offered her feelings, 'If Red doesn't take over, then someone else, but not Merrill, never Merrill.'

Hearing Edith and Grady whispering, Conchita wanted to scream out to them that Jim could not die. The unknown was putting a knife in her heart. What if Jim lives but doesn't remember her or want her? Life without Jim was unthinkable.

Edith said out loud, 'Who could have done this?'

No answer was given as they saw the patrol car speed up to the emergency entrance.

Several nurses and orderlies rushed out through the emergency room doors with a wheeled stretcher. They put Jim on the stretcher and transported him into the ER. Merrill and Red followed.

Conchita stood with Edith and Grady, looking into the emergency room while the doors were open.

An hour later, Red emerged with a grim look on his face.

He spoke to no one in particular. 'Jim's alive, but the doctor says it is touch and go. We will know more in the next twenty-four to forty-eight hours.'

Edith and Grady hugged each.

Conchita clutched her heart as she slowly collapsed into a waiting room seat. She became limp with the joy of knowing Jim was alive, for now. She couldn't talk, even if she'd wanted to, and who would she speak to. Her real feelings remained locked inside her heart away from any prying eyes.

Edith was clasping her hands together, walking around the waiting room, her face drawn and wan, looking everywhere and nowhere. Grady was standing at the exit door, lighting a cigarette, when Marlene and several deputies rushed in, looks of fear and apprehension on their faces.

Marlene looked around. Taking charge, she asked everyone, 'Is there any news about Sheriff Cobb?'

Red answered, 'He's alive, but he's critical.'

A sigh of relief came from the new arrivals. Everyone was nervous and anxious, some were sitting, others wandered around the room lost, while a few found the large coffee urn in the corner of the room.

Conchita was sitting alone, away from everyone else.

Silently she took out her rosary and prayed.

The waiting room became quiet. They spoke in hushed voices, as people gathered in twos and threes, worried and waiting for the next bit of information to come from the doctor.

The doctor came out in his surgical shirt, pants, and hat, a cotton mask pulled down from his face.

In a clear and direct voice, he said, 'Good evening, everyone, I'm Dr. Thomas, Jim Cobb's surgeon. The sheriff sustained a gunshot wound to his head, causing a linear skull fracture resulting in blood loss, unconsciousness, and a concussion. Fortunately, the bullet did not enter his brain. The cold night, up in the forest, slowed down his blood loss to next to nothing and enabled him to survive. He will need rest and quiet for the next several days to allow the wound to heal. His only visitors will be family.'

Thomas turned and left, not allowing any questions. Everyone looked at each other with relief on their faces, gathering their things to leave. Merrill shook hands with everyone as they left.

Only Red, Merrill, and Conchita remained. Merrill went over to where Conchita was sitting, holding her rosary. He bent and said, 'Conchita, you can visit with Jim. He looks upon you as family.'

CHAPTER 60

Shrouded in semi darkness, the hospital room was deathly silent in the night, only the beeping of machines saying the sheriff was breathing and his heart was beating. Some filtered illumination from the hall showing through the partially opened door. The sheriff had been brought into the hospital six hours earlier. A deputy was stationed outside Jim's room for 24-7 protection.

Conchita, the only visitor in the private room, sat next to Jim, holding his right hand with both of hers. His head was wrapped and bandaged with several layers of white gauze.

Conchita looked at Jim in silence. A single tear streaked down her cheek and finally fell on the hospital sheet creating a wet circle. She kept praying in silence in her native Spanish. She used the Catholic prayers she learned as a child in Mexico, willing the only man she ever wanted in her life to live.

Merrill came into the room and watched Conchita moving her lips in silence. Continuing to hold Jim's hand, she crossed herself, signifying the end of her devotion.

She looked up and saw Merrill. 'I'm leaving the ranch for good. I will move my things out tomorrow and go to my sister's house'

Merrill was so shocked he didn't respond, sitting in the chair she just vacated.

Conchita left Jim's room with her head held high, a purpose in her step.

Red came in just as Conchita was going out. Red liked her, maybe he should have asked her out, thinking they could have had a life together.

Jim didn't wake up that day or the next. He was trapped in a netherworld, unable to speak or follow directions. However, he was able to hear the chatter of the people who surrounded him, encouraging him to survive.

There were nurses going in and out of Jim's room, checking his vital signs, turning him in his bed, adjusting pillows under his head or next to his body, and replacing the bandage surrounding his head. Activity in the room was constant, like a beehive, always working, getting everything, just right. It wasn't every day the hospital had a celebrity or on this day, the most important person in the country, the sheriff.

Jim Cobb's survival depended on rest. Later he would have to think clearly about who shot him and left him for dead at Barton Haskel's cabin.

The bigger questions remained.

Who knew he was going to the cabin? Who killed Barton? The same person? What motive did the killer have?

CHAPTER 61

As Jim lay semi-conscious in his hospital bed, Conchita packed her meager belongings in a cardboard suitcase, readying for her departure to her sister Rosita's.

Minerva and Lottie were sitting in their living room alone. The ranch house and barn were silent as each woman drank cheap rye whiskey straight from old jelly glasses.

'What are we going to do if Jim Cobb dies?' asked Lottie.

Minerva told Lottie, 'We will find another way to get the law chasing after Silas's ass and put the bastard in jail.'

They heard the back door open, and the sisters looked at the other, not knowing who came in. The floor creaked as Silas approached the doorway and entered.

He looked worn out, wearing a scraggily beard, his clothes dirty, the odor of sweat permeating the air around him.

'Where the fuck are you hiding Woody?' he demanded.

'We haven't seen the boy in the past couple of days. He wanders in and out, never telling us what he's up to,' came the answer from Lottie. She had a handkerchief in her hands and scrunched it up in a nervous habit, looking around the room and not at Silas directly.

Silas picked up the Mellow Rye whiskey bottle and poured a jelly glass full. He drank half the glass in one swallow to get a quick hit of the alcohol and then took a sip, allowing the rye mash taste to run over his tongue before swallowing. Thinking about Lottie's answer, concerning Woody's whereabouts, he silently finished his drink.

Silas looked at the two women, the room, furniture, and surroundings with contempt. The life Silas had envisioned back in Oklahoma, before he killed his daddy, didn't include a life of meager wages, and robbing people of wealth from Hollywood. He didn't see himself living in a house inhabited by Minerva, Lottie, and Woody, either. He never knew what he wanted, but for him, this wasn't it.

Barton Haskel was dead, and Silas would now deal with Darren Harris directly, setting up the robberies, getting his fair share. Woody's involvement was still up in the air. Silas pored another half glass of whiskey and drank it. He stomped out of the room, leaving Minerva and Lottie worried about why he wanted to find Woody.

Suddenly, he came back in. 'Tell Woody to come to Barton Haskel's place,' he said, before leaving again.

The sisters were more bewildered than ever. They each feared what Silas had in store for Woody. Questions filled their minds:

Why Barton's place? What was Silas up to?

CHAPTER 62

Woody came through the back door into Barton Haskel's kitchen the next day around noon. Darren and Silas were sitting at the table having coffee.

'Well here's my good for nothing nephew. Say hello to Darren, the boss of this here enterprise,' said Silas.

Woody and Darren said hello to each other while Silas drank his coffee.

'Have a seat, Woody.' Darren drained his coffee cup. 'Your uncle and I have been discussing the future of the Cowboy Bar & Grill, along with our other financial ventures.'

Woody hadn't known his uncle Silas had been robbing Hollywood types with the help of Barton Haskel and Darren Harris. Woody never knew where Silas got the money he had. The boy never saw his uncle work. His mother and aunt never asked Silas where he got the paltry amount of money he gave them.

The only thing Woody knew about his dear old uncle was he had hung the man in the barn over by Bishop a couple of weeks ago. Silas had taken Woody along to watch the festivities. He was grooming Woody to take over the family's other business. Woody was to become the Hanging Murderer heir apparent.

Woody sat in silence with his back to the outside door.

'Let me assure you both, nothing has changed since Barton's death. I will tell you who to rob, where they are staying, and what specifically, other than money, you will take. Woody, your job is to work at the Cowboy Bar & Grill with Juan, as the busboy, sweeper, and all-around handyman. I will come up from Los Angeles when I know who is coming to make a movie or TV show.'

They looked at Darren like he was the teacher at the head of a one room schoolhouse. They never questioned anything he said, nodding their heads in agreement to each word he uttered. 'Woody, you and Silas will rob the people as I instruct you

to do, and leave the stolen goods at Barton's cabin in the Inyo Forest. Understand?'

Silas took over and answered for himself and Woody. 'Yes, we understand, Mr. Harris. What do you think we are, a couple of fucking idiots?'

Harris smiled at the little man, smelling the disgusting bitter odor coming off his unwashed clothes. There wasn't anything else to say to the two crooks.

Nobody offered information about Barton Haskel's death. And neither Silas nor Woody said anything to Darren about the Hanging Murders.

As far as they both were concerned, their form of status quo was back in place.

CHAPTER 63

I sat up a little in my hospital bed, my head hurting like hell. The nurse informed me that I'd been in the hospital for seventy-two hours, drifting in and out of consciousness. Merrill and Conchita had taken turns sitting with me the entire time. Now that I was awake, more people from the office wanted to visit.

A bandage covered my ears, forehead, skull, and upper neck, and I felt like my head was entombed. My vision was fine, but my hearing was muffled, until I heard a distinctive croaky voice, out in the hallway, that deep hoarse timbre, which could only be Marlene.

'I'm going back to the sheriff's office. Anyone need a ride?' she asked.

Edith, my first non-family visitor, came into my hospital room. 'I'm so glad you're awake, Jim, we were all worried about you since finding out you were shot.' Edith looked around the room as she caught her breath, 'I need to tell you, Grady called his editor about the shooting and they want a complete story with all the details.'

She looked directly into my eyes, wanting confirmation that I would grant an interview to her boyfriend.

I thought to myself, if the asshole wants an interview, then why doesn't he ask himself? I looked at Edith. She seemed nervous, holding her hands and rubbing them together, not knowing what to do next. Finally, she relaxed. She had other news to deliver. 'Jim, I have to tell you about the anonymous calls Grady has been receiving. Someone keeps calling and telling him to stop writing about the murders in Lone Pine.'

I didn't want to tell her that Grady was only with her for the stories she might tell him. The bastard would leave her when his latest article graced the pages of the *Los Angles Post* or some other rag. The man wrote gossip about movie starlets. It wasn't like he wrote the *Grapes of Wrath* or something. I wished she could find someone local to care for, not this so-called journalist.

This babble from Edith was becoming tiring. I just wanted to go back to sleep. Merrill and Red came into my room, hearing the last of Edith's words in favor of her latest sweetheart. My father and Red ushered her out of the room. She was headed back to her house and Grady.

I was drifting in and out of sleep when Juan came rushing into my room. He told my father and Red that he had something to tell them about Silas Reid. Merrill, who never relied on any Mexican's story as being true, told Juan to come back tomorrow, when I was awake.

Juan insisted, 'Señor Reid came into the Cowboy and said he was in charge. I'm afraid of him, Sheriff Cobb.'

Red answered him. 'It's okay, Juan, the department will look into it.'

Juan, unsure of the answer, left the hospital room with the weight of the world on his shoulders.

With all the people in and out, where was Conchita? She was the only person I wanted in my room, her expressive look of safety captured by her nurturing actions was all I wanted. The woman had no idea the power she had over me.

Darkness clouded my mind and body into slumber.

CHAPTER 64

The fourth day following the shooting, Merrill and Red came into my hospital room just after ten a.m. I was up and sitting in a chair. The nurse had just left after redressing my head wound with a more modest bandage.

'There were no clues up at the cabin, Jim.' Red looked frustrated. 'It snowed off and on, most of the time since you were shot, covering any tracks. We had men up there scouring the area. We'll find the bastard, if it's the last thing the sheriff's department does.'

I smiled. 'That's good to hear. Any other news, anything from the DOJ or FBI?'

Red was back in his element. 'Both have coordinated and sent information about the Hanging Murders to state police, county sheriff's offices, and local police in California, Arizona and Nevada. Nothing has come in yet.'

'Tell him the other news, Red,' Merrill added.

'I'm getting to it,' Red shot a look at Merrill before he continued. 'The LAPD found a fence for some of the stolen property from the Hollywood people. The fence said he never heard of anyone named Sailor or the name of an accomplice in the sale of the items.'

Merrill interjected, 'I'll bet my pension on Darren Harris having his hands in the robberies. He knew the Hollywood people who came up here.'

I nodded, but it hurt my head. I'd have to remember not to do that again any time soon. 'I'm sure you're right about Harris. Any news about Haskel's ties to Mendota?'

Red detailed the facts. 'The information from the Fresno County sheriff concerning Barton's family in Mendota said John Gates had lived in the home but no family relationship was established. Russell was a younger half-brother to Barton, who lived with the mother until he joined the Marines in December 1941. He died in the final battle of Guadalcanal.'

I knew all that but I had no reason not to listen.

'The mother learned of Russell's death from the Marine Corps and went on a bender. After seven days the neighbors found her dead, alone in her living room. The FBI found out that Gates returned from the war in 1946, after several operations in England. The people interviewed in Mendota said Barton and he were close growing up.'

Merrill added. 'I remember that Barton was rejected by the army because of a heart murmur.'

I told them about my interview with Gates. 'When I talked to John Gates in Banning, he never mentioned his relationship with Barton. The picture I showed him of Barton with two other men resulted in a negative response. I watched his face, he didn't even bat an eye.'

Red asked, 'Could Barton and Gates have been related somehow in Mendota?'

'I don't know,' I replied. 'It looks like I need to have another talk with John Gates.'

'Not for a while, you don't,' Red said, then left the room.

I'm sure Merrill told Red he wanted some time to talk with me in private.

'Conchita moved out of the ranch and is living at her sister's house,' said Merrill. 'I'm going to find a housekeeper for the ranch. To cook and clean for us when you are able to get out of this hospital room.'

I didn't respond to the news about Conchita.

CHAPTER 65

After informing Juan about Woody working at the Cowboy Bar & Grill, Darren went to Barton's house. He picked up the phone and placed a long distance call to John Gates in Banning. The phone rang seven times before Gates finally picked up.

'John, I want you to stay in Banning running The Red Caboose for the time being. I have Silas Reid's idiot nephew up here working at the Cowboy as a busboy while I set up some more robberies. I want to see if this new setup works out. If it doesn't, I'll need you to come back here.'

'Got it. If you want me to resolve Silas and the nephew, give me a call. I can be up there in a few hours and still have a solid story for me here in Banning.'

Darren smiled. 'I'll keep that in mind. I do have another question. Have you heard anything about this newspaper reporter, Grady Bennett, from the *LA Post*?'

'I heard of him, that's all,' Gates replied. 'Why?'

'He's writing about Barton and the Hanging Murders. Do you know of any connection?'

'No, Barton never talked about the murders. I don't know if he knew who was doing the killing or not.'

Darren said, 'I may need you to take care of the reporter, plus Reid, and also his nephew. This reporter may look further into the robberies, including me, and my relationship with Barton.'

Gates asked, 'What could he find?'

'That's none of your business. I don't want anyone looking at me or my history in Hollywood.'

'Okay, whatever you want, Darren. I'm ready whenever you call. I'll be quiet about anything you want done.'

'I'll call when I need you to solve my problem.'

Darren hung up and contemplated his new working relationship with Silas and Woody. Like Barton, he didn't really trust Silas and was determined to always keep an open eye, watching the little ferret. Calling on John Gates to solve any problems in Lone Pine seemed like a satisfactory option.

The reporter would be dealt with if he caused any more trouble.

CHAPTER 66

Since my release from the hospital four days before, I'd just been sitting at home, antsy and bored to death. Merrill hired a woman to cook for us at the ranch. She was in her sixties and had never cooked for anyone other than herself.

After dinner the night before I was supposed to be going back to work, I said, 'Dad, this woman you hired? She has to go. She can't cook, her hearing is so bad I have to yell, and she doesn't clean the kitchen.'

'I understand. She's finished. I'll find someone else.'

I smiled at my father's acceptance of the inevitable. 'Any news of who shot me? Or on the local murders?'

Merrill replied, 'No news on you or the Hanging Murderer. Barton's killer is an unknown, too. Questions concerning Gates down in Banning are on hold.'

The front doorbell rang. Merrill answered and it was Dave Finn from forensics.

'Come in, Dave. Want some coffee?' 'That would be good.'

We sat at the table after Merrill poured Dave a cup of coffee.

'Any information on the person who shot me?' I asked.

Dave fixed his coffee and informed us, 'All we know is the shooter used a .22 caliber round.' Merrill glanced at me as Dave continued. 'The forensic boys found the bullet, embedded in the wall across the main room of the cabin. The collective thought is you turned your head just enough for the bullet to hit your head, causing the fracture without entering the brain. A half inch more and we would be going to your funeral. In our office we've nicknamed you the cat, with one less life.'

I looked at my dad and we both laughed.

'The shooter wasn't much of a hunter, using a .22. If he was,' I said, 'I would have expected a larger caliber bullet.'

Merrill noted, 'This is the worse coffee I've ever tasted.'

We all laughed. I threw my napkin at him. 'I'm going to bed.'

'Good night, Jim. I'll drive us to the office tomorrow after we stop for breakfast.'

Merrill let Dave out the front door and turned out the lights before heading to bed.

The next morning, after breakfast in Independence at the Morning Cup coffee shop, Merrill and I returned to the cruiser. I told him, 'Tomorrow I'll drive myself to work.'

Merrill looked at me, didn't reply, backed up, and drove to the sheriff 's office.

My entrance into the station was greeted with well wishes and questions of how I was feeling on my return to work. I went into my office and saw Red sitting in front of my desk. My head bandage was now reduced to one large piece of gauze and tape.

I sat down at my desk. 'Let's start with who and where is Darren Harris?'

Merrill came into my office with two cups of coffee; he set one in front of me. I told him and Red, 'I'm going down to Banning tomorrow to talk with Gates.'

'We have a few other avenues to follow,' Red noted. 'I'll get a warrant to look at Barton's bank records.'

'Good, Red. Also, look into who owned Barton's house and the cabin where I was shot. Talk with Sheriff Deis in Fresno County about any other ties in Mendota.'

Merrill volunteered, 'I'll get in touch with the LAPD about the fence who sold the items stolen from people visiting us here in Lone Pine. Maybe I can get a line on who's the accomplice in the robberies.'

Before Red left my office, he said, 'Chief Huntly called while you were recovering in the hospital. He said the autopsy on Lara Aartz indicated a suicide. Veronal, a barbiturate, was in her system, she had a prescription from a local doctor. Her prescription was for forty pills and the bottle was empty.

'All right, that answers that. My last next question is, who tried to kill me and why?'

CHAPTER 67

Red had contacted the FBI and state DOJ for any news concerning the murders—Barton's and the Hanging Murders. The FBI and DOJ called late in the day returning Red's call with nothing new. My office was now quiet after a long day.

I left at seven and went to see Conchita at her sister's house outside of Lone Pine.

I knocked three times and Rosita opened the door. I was ready to ask about Conchita when she pointed down the hall, to the farthest bedroom, without saying a word. My mouth was still partially open as I went down the hall.

I needed to take a deep breath before softly tapping on the bedroom door. No sound resonated from the room. It felt like I was standing there for an eternity, my mind making up countless scenarios. She wasn't inside. She was asleep. She didn't want to see me. I was still flashing through the possibilities when the door opened a crack. All I saw was a single obsidian colored eye looking in my direction.

I smiled as the door opened completely, revealing Conchita. Neither of us said a word as we slipped into each other's arms, as though this was the most natural occurrence on earth. I kicked the door closed.

I didn't care who else in the house knew I had entered the bedroom. I was inside now, with the one person I wanted to be with since my return from the war. This revelation struck me like lightning. How had I never figured it out until this very minute?

We released each other from our first embrace, taking a half step back, but still touching. I looked into Conchita's eyes. I didn't want to disrupt the spell I was feeling.

Conchita put her index finger to my lips, requesting no words. She grasped my hand and led me to the side of her bed.

Conchita put her hands on each side of my face, our lips barely brushed one another before she stood on her tip toes and covered my mouth with hers.

She tasted like cinnamon and vanilla. It felt real but seemed like a dream. I needed air and pulled my head back.

I felt unsteady and held on tightly to her waist. She smiled, looking at me with an impish glance, signaling what she wanted. She sat on the bed and pulled me down beside her.

I looked into her eyes. 'Conchita, I wanted you from the first day we met, but I couldn't…'

She interrupted me by kissing me deeply.

The fire in my body was burning for her. She let out a pleased gasp and smiled as I pushed her back and gently glided on top of her.

I wanted to enjoy the moment, not rush through like a seventeen-year-old on his first big date. I'd been married for thirteen years. I knew all the parts on both sides of the aisle, I wanted this woman, but I needed her to want equally.

Lifting my head, I looked into her eyes. 'Conchita, I want to be with you. I want to go slow. I want to know everything, from before you came to America. What you like and don't. Who you are. What do you want in your life? I have so many questions I want ask.'

'Shush, shush, my love,' Conchita whispered as she put a finger across my lips, 'All in good time, my Jim, we can take it slow, make us each happy. I want to give myself to you. I never knew a man who wanted me for myself, nothing more.'

She kissed me softly before saying, 'I came here, worked for your mother, but when I first saw you, I knew deep in my soul. I stopped breathing when I saw you. My heart broke when Harriet made you small in your marriage. I wanted to rip her eyes out, I hated her, and what she didn't want, you to run for sheriff.'

'Yes, she had her own agenda,' I replied. 'She didn't want a life with me and Kendall or to live here in the high desert.'

Conchita smiled. 'I'll stay here with you for however long you want me.'

We kissed again as I relaxed in her arms. I was safe, secure in the bosom of the woman I loved.

We didn't need more words tonight. There would be time enough for us to grow together. We embraced.

We made love until the morning light sneaked past the curtains. I knew this was where I needed to be, and who I wanted to spend the rest of my life with, us together.

I was finally home.

CHAPTER 68

I strode into the Cowboy Bar & Grill a little after two in the afternoon. The lunch crowd was thinning out as I made my way back to the kitchen. Juan was standing at the grill; he'd just turned over a burger and placed a slice of American cheese on top and moving the soft bun around as it browned on the grill next to the burger. As I watched, he took out steak fries from the deep fryer to drain on the wire rack.

'How you doing, Señor Jim?'

'Fine. And you?' I looked around the kitchen. 'Bien,' Juan replied.

'I came to ask where your boss is.'

Juan said sadly, 'You already know. Señor Barton, está muerto.'

'No, not him. I'm asking about the real boss, Darren Harris.'

Juan stopped in mid-action for a couple of seconds before he placed the bottom of the toasted bun on the white oval plate, followed by the burger with the melted cheese. A ladle of chili sauce from a pot simmering on the stove was put on top of the cheese. The top of the toasted bun was placed face up next to the burger. He then put a raw slice of red onion and a half inch thick slab of a fresh Brandywine tomato on the bun. He sprinkled coarse salt and pepper on the tomato and picked up the basket with the drained steak fries from over the deep fryer and shuffled them out onto the plate. Almost finished with the order, he added a quarter-wedge of full-length kosher dill pickle from an open container and placed it between the burger and the fries without touching either one.

Putting the finished plate on the stainless-steel shelf he called out, 'Order up.' Then, almost mouthing the words, he said, 'Señor Jim, I'm scared of Silas Reid.' He was silent, hoping I'd forgotten all about asking him about Darren Harris.

'Why are you afraid of him?'

'When I came to live here, I first work for Señora Reid out at their ranch. He was always mean to her, hitting her and little Archie.' Juan swallowed, looking around, and nervously continued. 'I left after about a year and started cooking at the Roadhouse Cafe, before it burned down. I hated him for what he did to his family, but I did nothing to stop him.' He looked at me and took a deep breath. 'I did wrong?'

'No, Juan, it was none of your business. If you had done something at the time, some people around here would have hurt you, or run you out of town.'

He didn't respond to my assessment of the situation. I waited while he puttered around in the kitchen.

I gently reminded him why I was there. 'Tell me about Mister Harris, where is he?'

Juan was sweating and not from the heat in the kitchen. He turned and pointed with one finger to the closed back office door. 'I don't know any Señor Harris.'

I didn't want to give him away if anyone was listening to our conversation from the office, but understood his direction and pushed opened the office door and walked in. The man sitting behind the desk had a silver dollar size brown birthmark on the right side of his neck.

'Darren Harris, I'm Sheriff Jim Cobb of Inyo County.'

CHAPTER 69

I returned to my office and asked Red to come in.

'I met Darren Harris,' I said. 'He insisted that the writing on the note was by whoever killed Barton and called it all lies and untruths. He said he'd known Barton since the early thirties. He came up to Lone Pine around that time, working as a location scout for Majestic Pictures. Barton was working extra-time, as security, on a movie shoot when they met.'

I paused to let Red digest what I was telling him. 'Harris went on to say when Barton retired from the sheriff's department, he hired him to run the Cowboy Bar. This past summer, when they didn't get along, he sent Barton's half-brother, John Gates, down to Banning to run The Red Caboose Bar.'

'Half-brother?' Red laughed. 'So, they were related. And Darren Harris knew Haskel and Gates were related?'

'He knew. I'm sure Haskel requested Gates for the job as barkeep.'

'And then they got in a fight. What about Sailor?' Red asked.

'Harris said he never knew anyone named Sailor. He also said he didn't know about any robberies taking place in the area.'

'It seems Darren Harris wants us to come to a complete dead end, telling stories about the virtues of Haskel and Gates, without acknowledging the thefts from all the Hollywood people during that time,' said Red. 'He must have heard about the robberies from people in the movie business, or the local papers, or from Haskel.'

'I'm sure you're right. Who do you think he wants us to investigate?'

'I don't know, Jim. But,' Red smiled while answering, 'I think we should go have a talk with Lottie Pilgrim about everything Darren has said.'

'Excellent idea,' I replied with a grin.

Late November in Inyo County went through a short spell of warmer than usual days for this time of year. The aspen and birch trees had already turned gold and orange. They would eventually turn red before the leaves dropped off and blanketed the area before winter set in.

We rode out to the Reid ranch under a cloudless indigo sky with the temperature shooting up to the mid-eighties.

It was a spectacular day in the high desert.

CHAPTER 70

Archie and Reinhard were still at the Mount Whitney Motel in Lone Pine. Archie's plan of seeing Sheriff Jim Cobb about Silas being the Hanging Murderer fell flat with the news about the sheriff's shooting at Barton Haskel's cabin.

Archie decided, with helpful assistance from Reinhard, that the time had come for the two buddies to drive out to the ranch. If Silas was there, they would confront him. If he tried anything, there were two of them, and they would both tower over him, Archie knew. If he wasn't there—and Archie almost hoped he wouldn't be, then they would to find out if Minerva knew where he was. And make their decisions from there.

As they drove north from the Mount Whitney Motel, passing Independence, the sheriff's patrol car pass them on the highway, with two men in it, headed in the same direction.

Reinhard touched Archie's arm. 'Where do you think they're going? What's out here?'

'Not much, just my parents' ranch.'

Let's follow them, I'm curious to see if the sheriff is going there. Besides, it's a beautiful day for a drive.' He lit up a Camel. 'Tell me about Gretchen?'

Archie couldn't help smiling. 'She's wonderful. Growing up here and living with a father like mine made me wonder about ever finding someone to love and starting a family.'

'I know about your family, starting when you were talking in your nightmares, and from what you've told me. What about Gretchen?' Reinhard insisted.

'Well, I started driving for the winery about six years ago and met Gretchen a little while later. She worked in the bottling plant.' Archie smiled at the memory. 'I looked at her and the world stopped, I couldn't breathe, I couldn't talk, I couldn't even move. A guy bumped into me. I was a stump in the road.'

Reinhard punched Archie on the arm. 'Okay, I get it, she's beautiful…'

'No, she is more, Gretchen is more than that. Nice, sweet, kind, generous, and smart.' Archie stared straight ahead at the road, unable to talk.

'Reinhard to Archie, come in… what else is this wonder woman you live with?'

'I can't explain it, when we are together the rest of the world stops. I'll never introduce her to my family. Gretchen is the sun, the moon, and the stars, my family is the cow manure in the field.'

'I hope you let me meet her, Archie, I'm not your blood, but I'm all you got.'

'Reinhard, you are my brother, all the family I want or need.

I want you to be my best man at the wedding.'

'Hallelujah! God bless America, my only brother is getting married, and his bride is having their baby. God in heaven, this is a wonderful day!'

Archie laughed at his friend's comments, and wished this entire ordeal was over and finished. He wanted to get back to Modesto, to work, and most of all, to Gretchen. Archie wanted to feel her belly grow with his child inside.

Ahead of them, the sheriff's car turned into the driveway for the Reid house.

'That's the drive to my family's house,' Archie said. 'I was right. I knew it. Let's go.'

Talking to Jim was the last thing Archie wanted to do right then. He wasn't sure what he wanted to say. Or hear. He drove by the entrance and parked on the side of the road. 'What do you think the sheriff is doing, inside the house?'

'I don't know.'

'We can't just wait here.'

'Why don't we make it look like we are changing a flat until the sheriff leaves?' Reinhard suggested.

'Sounds like a plan, Reinhard.'

CHAPTER 71

Thirty minutes after Jim and Red left for the Reid place, Marlene, the dispatcher at the sheriff's office, took a call. The caller reported a fire at the deserted Atkinson Ranch, east of Bishop. Marlene was so engrossed in a story told to her by someone who'd heard the story from someone else, when the call about the fire came in.

If Marlene hadn't been so involved in the gossip she was repeating to Edith and had listened to the caller, she might have recognized the person's voice. She might have realized it was the same person who called about the Hanging Murder at the old Conroy Ranch. The call that Perry Rimmer went out on. Unfortunately, she didn't have a scintilla of interest about anyone other than herself, so she missed the caller's voice in the fragment of a windmill that was her mind, a circle in a spiral of her self-importance.

She called Jim on the two-way radio and reported the fire. 'Marlene, who is stationed at the patrol division up in

Bishop today?'

'Deputy Perry Rimmer is on duty,' she replied. 'Good. Send him out to the Atkinson Ranch.' 'Will do, Jim. Out.'

CHAPTER 72

Red and I arrived at the Reid ranch to interview Silas, Lottie and Minerva but the person we really wanted to talk to at that point was Lottie.

We were informed that Silas was not there and they did not know where he was. Whether I believed them or not, I hadn't quite decided. We were ushered inside by Minerva and sat in the living room.

I watched them both closely, Minerva and Lottie, as I asked, 'Did either of you know Lara Aartz?'

Minerva was silent. No reaction.

Lottie spoke. 'I know who she is, but I never met her.' I asked, 'Did Barton tell you about her?'

Lottie looked nervous when she spoke. 'Yes, Barton told me first, and after, Juan, the Mex cook at the Cowboy, who said her name to me.'

I stiffened at the slur. 'Do either of you know about the relationship between John Gates and Barton Haskel?'

'I never met John Gates, or ever went into the Cowboy Bar & Grill,' Minerva spit out with repugnance.

'I knew John Gates since he started working at the Cowboy until he left after he had a fight with Barton,' admitted Lottie.

'I asked if you know about a relationship between Barton and Gates.'

Lottie nervously answered, 'They each worked at the Cowboy. I never saw anything else.'

Looking her squarely in the eyes, I said, 'If I told you that they were half-brothers from Mendota, what would you say?'

'I'd say I never knew that. But so what?' Chin up, eyes narrowed, Lottie looked at me in defiance as she spoke. I sensed that she was hiding what she knew about the Cowboy Bar & Grill.

'Lottie, do you know what the fight between Barton and Gates was about?'

'No. I didn't see the fight or know anything about it,' Lottie replied, 'I just heard that John was fired and went down to Banning.'

I noted that she said John and not Gates. Red asked, 'Where's Silas and Woody?'

Minerva answered, 'Silas left, hunting, several days ago and Woody left a couple of days later. The child comes and goes without a word. God only knows what he does.'

'Was Silas working for Barton?' Red asked. 'Robbing Hollywood people when they worked up here at filming locations?'

'I don't know what Barton was doing, and I don't know anything about my Silas robbing anyone,' Minerva responded.

I moved on. 'Do either of you know anyone around here using the nickname Sailor?'

'Sheriff, we're a long way from the ocean,' Minerva scoffed. 'Now who would use a nickname like that? It would take a damn fool to call himself Sailor when there wasn't no water around.'

'That's right Minerva, but this person may have been given the name before he came here.' I stared straight at her.' Any ideas now?'

'No, Sheriff,' Minerva assured me. Then she looked at Lottie, her stern face, her eyes silently demanding her sister not to say a word.

'Okay.' I turned my attention from one woman to the other. 'Lottie, did you and Barton have a romantic relationship?'

Lottie took a deep breath. 'We went out to the movies a of times.' She paused, sniffling. 'After Barton met Lara Aartz, we never went out again.'

Lottie looked lost in her fantasy of the truth. I wanted to know what was behind her eyes and all the secrets she and Minerva possessed.

'Did you kill Barton Haskel?' I let my question implicate both sisters.

The response was emphatic from both. 'No!'

But my question stirred up some strange reactions. Minerva said, 'What a thing to ask, Sheriff.' But Lottie twitched in her chair, crumpling a handkerchief in her clutched hands.

Their reactions let me know these two were neck deep in knowing who Barton's murderer was. Getting them each in court and proving the fact was a long way off.

I motioned to Red that the interview was finished.

'Lottie, Minerva, that's all the questions for now. If I have any more, I'll come by and see you both. If you think of anything, you let me know.'

Minerva rose from her chair and paced around the room, looking at nothing.

Lottie was still crumpling the handkerchief. 'We don't have anything to hide, Sheriff,' she said. 'But I can't think of anything else you might need to ask us. We live out here alone. Now with Barton gone, I doubt that I will be going to the Cowboy again.' She looked lost.

Red and I both nodded our heads. 'Thanks,' I said.

We left the house, and as I started the patrol car, Marlene's voice came over the two-way. 'Sheriff, Perry Rimmer called from the Atkinson place. There's another Hanging Murder up there.'

CHAPTER 73

The wind had kicked up at the northern end of the county. Joanna, Rimmer's pregnant wife, was complaining that winter was coming too early and made the deputy keep a fire going in their woodstove all night.

This area east of Bishop was poor for farming and ranching. The abandoned Atkinson's ranch was isolated from the few others east of Bishop. This rugged location was only favorable to a few hardy souls who stuck it out in the worst of conditions.

The Atkinson family hadn't been one of the few.

The story among the locals was that the Atkinsons lasted about ten years before they packed it in and moved to the San Joaquin Valley. The ranch had been deserted ever since, or was thought to be.

The main ranch house had most of its windows broken out, the front door was off its hinges, and old, destroyed furniture was in each room. The place looked haunted, just like the old Conroy Ranch he had been called out to almost eight weeks before. Rimmer noticed an out-building on the other side of the barn, an area where a small fire had burned itself out. The wood used for the fire was only partially burned.

Rimmer made his way out to the barn. One of the doors was off the hinges and in a heap in front of the barn. The rest of the place was still standing, except for the east wall, which was broken down and destroyed by the weather.

As he went inside the Dutch gambrel roof end of the t-shaped structure, a small flock of black birds flew over his head, out of the opening. There was a little daylight in the back section of the barn. He heard nothing but the sound of the wind and the creaking of the worn out, old, wooden walls of the barn. His feared the remaining barn structure might fall on his head.

The central aisle had empty stalls with remnants of manure and straw on the hard dirt floor. The tack room was bare. There were cobwebs around the wooden pegs once used for rawhide harness hooks.

Rimmer continued to walk, with a foreboding sensation washing over him, as he neared the crossing aisle at the end of the central walkway. He looked to his right and saw the gambrel roof end section with missing wooden boards, allowing cloud covered light to pass over the empty aisle. Rimmer turned to the other end. That end was dark, requiring him to walk to the end of the corridor.

This Hanging Murder appeared exactly like the last one.

The body looked as if death had occurred a few days earlier. It swayed in the slight breeze, the rope holding the body to the rafter creaking with each movement.

Blackbirds had pecked out the man's eyes.

Perry Rimmer had served with the Army in Korea but had never seen the horrors of war up close. Now within eight weeks he had found two men killed in the most gruesome way. Hung, then pulled up by their ankles, with slashed throats, all the blood inside collected under their bodies. The inhumanity of the tragedy forced Rimmer to throw up again in an empty stall. Perry was cleaning himself up before calling in the murder scene. As the young deputy sat on his heels, he wrestled with continuing on with the sheriff's department. Inyo County, where he grew up and wanted to have a life in with his wife and soon to be child, had never seemed dangerous, until now.

Perry thought to himself, fish or cut bait? I've never left any job before. I'm not a coward. I'm not afraid. He was thinking of what his dad would say when he was growing up, 'Perry, pick yourself up and get back on that horse.' Perry remembered his dad as being 'black or white' about anything and everything. Dad had his ways but Perry knew that his dad was always in his corner.

Perry Rimmer did exactly what his dad wanted. He called in the murder and waited for the sheriff.

CHAPTER 74

Jim and Red heard the news from Marlene. Jim gunned the engine and streaked out of the Reid Ranch, with full siren and lights flashing, heading north.

The Pontiac with Archie and Reinhard were off to the side of the road just south of the ranch's entrance. The two men had indeed made it look like they were fixing a flat tire. Archie put the tire jack in the trunk.

'What could have happened?' Reinhold asked, worried. Archie was shaken. 'We need to get to the ranch right now!'

Minerva and Lottie were looking out the front window, after hearing the sheriff's patrol car tear out of there with the siren blaring.

Lottie asked, 'Why didn't you want me to tell the sheriff about Silas using Sailor as a nickname?'

'It will all come out in due time, little sister. Did I hear you talking about hoping Barton was going to be your next husband?'

A strange car drove up. Minerva saw the thin, muscular figure emerge from the driver's side. She started to cry as she leaned her face against the window glass.

Lottie came up beside her sister and put her arm around her. 'What's happening? Minerva, what's wrong?' Seeing two men walking up to the door, Lottie said, 'This has to be bad.'

'It's my boy,' Minerva replied through her sobs. 'He's come home.'

Lottie hadn't seen her nephew since he was an infant back in Oklahoma. She didn't know which young man, walking up the porch steps to the front door, could be Archie.

Archie knocked on the door, rattling the old oak. 'Mama, are you in there? It's Archie. Open the door.'

Reinhard stood behind his best friend.

Minerva composed herself and opened the door with tears in her eyes.

'Is that you, Archie, come home to see me?' She was beside herself, seeing her son for the first time in fifteen years. She wrapped her arms around his neck and cried.

'Is it really you, Archie, come home?' Minerva stepped away with tears running down her cheeks.

'Yeah, Mama, it's me.' He stood away and looked at his friend. 'Mama, this is my friend, Reinhard. We were in the army together.'

Minerva was wiping away the tears with the back of her hands, then wiped her hands on her apron and held out her hand. She wanted to backhand her son for all the grief he had caused her, not returning home after the war. Never writing her where he lived, what he was doing, and confiding in her what he wanted to make of his life. All the endless questions evaporated in an instant; Minerva just wanted to hold her only child in her arms.

Smiling, she said. 'Glad to meet ya, Reinhard.'

'The pleasure's all mine, Mrs. Reid.' Reinhard replied.

Lottie cleared her throat, signaling to Minerva that she was there.

Minerva remembered her sister standing next to her. 'Excuse me, boys,' she said, thrusting Lottie in front of Archie and Reinhard. 'This is my sister, Lottie. She's your aunt, Archie.'

Lottie shook hands with Reinhard, then hugged Archie tight. The introductions complete, Minerva said, 'Come on boys,

come in, let's sit in the living room and talk.'

'Where's Dad?' Archie asked, warily looking around.

'Not here,' Minerva said. 'He was here but he left, I don't know where he went.'

Archie and Reinhard sat in the seats just vacated by Jim and Red.

'Can I get you two some lemonade?' asked Lottie. 'It's fresh made today.'

Archie glanced at her and nodded. 'Sure, that would be swell. We'll each have a glass.'

Lottie left the room for the kitchen.

'Why were the cops just here?' Archie asked. 'We saw them tearing out of here, siren blaring.'

'They were asking the same question you just did, son. Where's Silas? But never mind that, Archie. Where are you living, what are you doing, do you have a wife or a girlfriend…?' Minerva trailed off, realizing her onslaught of questions might be too much for her son.

'I'm living in Modesto, driving a truck for a winery, and I have a girlfriend named Gretchen.' Archie needed to catch his breath after he rattled off the information.

'I'm so happy for you.' Crying, Minerva added, 'I've missed you so much, Archie, since you left for the war.'

'I know, Mama.'

'I got your letter after you came back, I keep it with my private things, and I read it every night.' Minerva looked at her son. 'I know why you didn't come home. I understand.'

'I wanted to, but not with Daddy here. He swore to me, before I left, he was never going to kill anyone else. I thought he kept his word. I didn't come back, thinking my staying away would keep him from starting again. Then I read about the murder last month, in the Modesto newspaper.'

'It made the papers all the way there?' Minerva looked to the window, wanting to end the talk about Silas. Uncontrollable tears started falling down her face.

'Mama, I need to find him.'

Frowning, Minerva replied, 'I honestly don't rightly know for sure where he is right now.'

Archie asked, 'Don't you have any idea at all, Mom?'

Lottie returned with two glasses of cold lemonade, 'Here you go, boys. Drink up, it's good and cold. I couldn't help but overhear your question, Archie.' Not looking at Minerva, she bit her lip before continuing. 'I think my boy, Woody, went off with Silas to Barton Haskel's cabin up in the mountains.'

Minerva glared at her sister. The last thing she wanted was Archie and his friend going up to that cabin.

Hoping she knew, Archie asked, 'Can you tell us how to get there, Aunt Lottie?'

Since Lottie had met Barton there many times, Archie and Reinhard received detailed directions to the cabin.

'Is that where the sheriff was going?' Reinhold asked.

'I don't think so,' Lottie said. 'The sheriff got a call about a fire and they rushed off.'

Both men went to the door. Minerva threw her arms around her son's neck, kissing him on his face. 'Archie, tell me you'll come back and bring Gretchen next time.'

'Yes, Mama, we'll come back real soon.' Archie pulled his mother's arms away from his neck.

'Promise me, Archie, promise!' Minerva pleaded. 'Life isn't endless, you know.'

'I know.' Archie looked into his mother's frantic face. 'I promise, real soon.'

Leaving was becoming difficult. Reinhard held the door for Archie.

'Be careful!' Minerva called after them. 'Both of you!'

CHAPTER 75

Perry Rimmer stood next to his car and waited for the patrol car with Jim and Red to stop. 'I called it in to Marlene. She says to tell you the FBI, state DOJ evidence team are on the way. The mortuary is sending someone, and patrols from Bishop are on their way.'

'Thanks, Perry.' Jim looked around. 'Show us what you found.'

Perry led them into the barn to the area with the murdered man. The body was in the same position as all the other Hanging Murders, hung from his feet with hands and feet restrained, neck cut, with what looked like his entire blood supply drained on the ground below the head, and most likely murdered by hanging first with the cutoff remnant of rope still around the victim's neck.

Red searched the immediate area for evidence.

Jim looked at the victim, not recognizing the dead man. 'Perry,' he said, 'tell me about the rest of the property and the ranch house.'

'Abandoned for years. The house has no signs of any inhabitants for a long time, broken furniture throughout. No food or living supplies in sight. The fire in the other building was set to get someone out here and it burned itself out. There was no real damage . The person who set the fire knew what he was doing. He started it with a book of matches and a long, slow fuse that ran over five-hundred yards from the outbuilding. He set the blaze a couple of days ago, from the look of it.'

As Perry was talking, Jim noticed the edge of a piece of paper in the victim's back pocket. He pulled it out with his fingertips, hoping to find something that might lead them to the killer or killers. Jim realized the paper came from a larger pad. He turned it over and saw the name, SILAS, written in block capital letters.

Red, looking over Jim's shoulder, said, 'It looks like the person involved was Silas Reid. Or someone wants us to think Silas is involved.'

Nodding, Jim said, 'That's how I read it, Red. We need to find Silas, or rule him out and find the killer. Let's head back to the Reid Ranch and ask Minerva a few more questions.'

Red pointed to the front of the barn and they both saw the deputies walking through the front entrance. They heard other vehicles driving into the yard. Red instructed his newly arrived deputies to follow orders from the FBI. He told Perry to follow the sheriff's patrol car to the Reid place.

'Call the station and have a few deputies meet us at the Reid Ranch, Red,' Jim said, preparing for a showdown. Tell them to stay outside if they arrive before we do.'

Jim drove back to the Reid's Ranch just about as fast as he had left it.

CHAPTER 76

Two cars, with a total of four deputies, were already parked outside. We marched up to the front door.

I banged of the door with side of my fist. 'Open up, it's Sheriff Cobb,' I shouted.

Lottie opened the door, 'Sheriff, what's wrong? What happened?'

'Ladies,' I said, 'we need to know the whereabouts of Silas and Woody.'

'I told you, Sheriff,' Minerva said, 'when you came before, we don't know where they are. Honest.'

'Minerva, we found another Hanging Murder at the abandoned Atkinson ranch. In the victim's back pocket was a piece of paper with Silas's name written on it.'

Minerva sat down in a chair, stone-faced.

Lottie kind of fell into the same chair she'd been sitting in when we were there before, next to her sister, twisting the handkerchief in her hands into a ball.

Glancing over at Minerva, I asked Lottie, 'Where's Woody, where's your son, Lottie?'

Lottie started to whimper. 'This morning he told me that his Uncle Silas went to Barton Haskel's hunting cabin yesterday,' she said. 'Woody was going up there with food and other provisions for his uncle.'

Red was exasperated. 'Why didn't you say that when we were here before, woman?' he demanded.

'I was afraid for my son's life if you caught up with them. God only knows what Silas would do if the police cornered him.'

'Lottie,' I said, 'I can arrest you for impeding a criminal investigation.'

Minerva chipped in. 'W…w…we're trying to save Woody's life. Silas is evil, we don't ever know what he will do.'

Headed for the door, I told Red. 'Have a deputy bring these two the station. Everyone else will need to drive up to Barton's cabin. Follow us. Let's hope we're in time.'

'Wait, Sheriff,' Lottie said, 'there's one more thing to tell you about today. Minerva's son, Archie, came to here with a war buddy of his, and they're driving up to the cabin right now.'

Clenching my fist, I took a deep breath and asked, 'How long ago did they leave?'

'Just before you came back,' Lottie replied, looking worried.

'Lottie, do you ever tell the truth?' I asked.

Lottie didn't answer, she looked down at the floor, hiding in plain sight, like a little girl.

'I don't think you ever tell the truth, Lottie. I'll get to the bottom of all your lies, misdirection, and complicity in this case.'

I turned and strode out.

CHAPTER 77

The Inyo County sheriff's vehicles followed my patrol car. We arrived at Barton's hunting cabin. The officers jumped out and surrounded the place, guns drawn, and I motioned for Red to go up to the front door. I had my .38 Smith out and ready.

I nodded to Red, standing back from the side of the door. He knocked twice with the side of his fist. 'Inyo County Sheriff! Open the door, Silas!' he shouted.

No response came from inside.

Red shouted again. 'Silas Reid, come out unarmed with your hands in the air!'

Nothing. He turned the doorknob and pushed the door open, placing his back against the outside wall, away from the door jam. A single rifle shot rang out, hitting the door jam.

Red instantly crouched down, a smaller silhouette for the shooter inside the cabin. He called out, 'We have the cabin surrounded! Come on out, Silas!'

Another rifle shot threw a piece of the door jamb in the air where Red's head had just been. The wood splintered and fell on Red. A single shot, and broken glass, was heard from the back of the cabin. I knew this had to come from Perry, who I'd directed to the northeast corner.

'I hit him in the shoulder!' Perry cried out. 'Clear to enter the cabin. I have the shooter covered and I'm walking up to the back of the cabin.'

The bullet had torn through Silas's right shoulder, forcing him to drop his rifle and grab his injured arm, writhing in pain. A deputy sheriff handcuffed Silas.

Woody Pilgrim was found hung, like all the other Hanging Murders, from the rafters in the bedroom, his throat cut from ear to ear. The boy's death had occurred only a short time before, the congealed blood under his head was still sticky.

'Why did you kill your nephew?' I demanded.

'The little fucker told me my days were over, he put a piece of paper with my name on it in the back pocket of the last guy up at the Atkinson Ranch. I don't know if he did or didn't, but that's what he told me.'

'He did,' I said.

Silas smiled as he looked over his handy work. 'He stabbed me in the back with that note. My own flesh and blood.'

The police searched the cabin and found an account book of sorts, with dates and amounts, and notes, written by Barton Haskel. It told all about meeting up with Silas Reid in 1932, the deal with Darren Harris, even his love for Lara Aartz. The final entry included and the setup with his half-brother John Gates to make everyone in town think they hated each other.

In Silas's truck outside, Perry found a box containing the most recent stolen items.

I was sick about Woody's death, and upset about who the man I thought was my best friend really was. But then I has to laugh—what better way to break the law than to get close to the lawman?

Before a deputy put Silas into a patrol car for the ride to the hospital to get care for the rifle wound to his shoulder, I asked him why he killed Barton Haskel. 'Why kill him?'

'Sheriff, you've got that all wrong,' he told me, wincing in pain. 'I never killed Haskel. We were partners. We didn't trust each other, but Barton was the key to all the robberies in Lone Pine. Why would I kill the golden goose?'

'Then who killed him?' I demanded.

'I wish I knew,' Silas said and somehow, I believed him.

As they were getting ready to put Silas in the back of a patrol car, I saw a Pontiac pull up. Two men got out.

Silas saw Archie. 'Finally, my long lost, fucking worthless, bastard son has returned home!' he yelled out. 'What the fuck are you doing here?'

Archie stammered, 'I came back because of the return of the Hanging Murderer I read about in the paper. I came back to turn you in to the sheriff. And myself, too.'

I looked at him sadly. The last time I'd seen him was before the war,' I said. 'It looks like Silas is the Hanging Murderer. His last victim was your cousin, Woody Pilgrim.'

'Noooo…' Archie wailed. 'Oh, God, Sheriff, I should have come to see you when I first arrived in Lone Pine and told you the complete story of what Silas did to me, my mother, and the murder victims.'

'I wish you had; it might have saved lives. Why didn't you?'

Archie said, 'I was afraid. I've been afraid of my father since I was a little kid. I'm still afraid. Now that you have him under arrest, I can tell you everything, I know you have to arrest me for what I did, but I want to confess and serve my time.'

CHAPTER 78

Before being taken to the hospital, Silas told Jim that Darren Harris had been staying at Barton's house for the last three or four days. Red sent Perry and two other deputies to Barton's house in Lone Pine, to arrest Darren for his involvement with Haskel and Reid, for the robberies of all the Hollywood people since 1932.

When Perry and the other deputies arrived, they found Darren was gone. Nothing was left behind. No clothes or personal items. No papers, no indication of where Darren went or if he left with anyone. If was like Harris went up in a puff of smoke.

A forensic team went to Barton's house and found fingerprints galore, but nothing of substance. All the known parties left their prints at the house. Back at the sheriff's office, Red was annoyed by the news. He said, 'Jim, Harris is gone in the wind.'

Nodding, Jim responded, 'Call LAPD, ask them to search Harris's house and office at the movie studio, interview any friends, coworkers, and employees. Put out an APB on Harris to all western states and Mexico.'

Merrill stalked into Jim's office, madder than a hornet. 'Jim, good you caught Silas. But what the hell happened to Harris?'

'Dad, we just missed Harris at Barton's house, but we are putting out a wide search, with the help of the FBI, state police, local law enforcement, and Mexico. We will find him.'

Red came in. 'I can't believe we missed Harris. I thought if Harris was caught, everything would be tied up in a nice, neat bow.'

'Unfortunately,' Merrill put in, 'life doesn't always end up in a clean nice, neat bow.'

Jim had the Hanging Murderer in jail. The man who organized and directed the robberies had left town. Darren Harris would eventually be found—the LAPD and the FBI were all on the lookout for the elusive Hollywood producer. Minerva and Lottie were brought in for questioning. The scales of justice seemed to balance in the right direction.

Jim said, 'Red, put Minerva and Lottie in separate interview rooms. Keep Archie and his army buddy here, we need to hear their story.'

Merrill decided to get some coffee.

Red stuck his head in. 'Sheriff, the ladies are in separate interview rooms.'

'Thanks, I'll be right there,' Jim answered.

He took one interview room while Red took the other and after an hour they switched. Two hours later, Red sat in the chair in front of the desk as Jim took his seat.

'What do you think, Red?'

'These two sisters are polecats who would eat their young.

But there's nothing to charge them with.'

'I came to the same conclusion. I would like to keep them in jail, just on general principle, but we don't have enough evidence of a crime. Lying to the sheriff is not enough for a conviction. Let them go. All we can hope is that coming down here and getting interviewed put the fear of God in their minds. Bring Archie and his friend in here.'

Edith brought in another chair. The room was crowed, stuffy, and getting hot from bodies and sweat.

Jim was direct. 'Archie, I can arrest you for aiding and abetting in the course of a murder. Silas and you could die together in San Quentin.'

Archie sat shriveled in his chair, looking like a ten-year-old in the principal's office.

Before he responded, Reinhard stepped in, 'Sheriff, I know you have every right to arrest Archie, but I heard all the stories when he cried out in his nightmares during the war. I could tell he was forced by a worthless father into doing things he would never do, if given the choice.'

Jim had to admire Reinhold for trying to save his buddy.

Reinhard took a breath. 'He won't tell you this, but Archie is a real war hero, he won a Bronze Star at Bastogne and a Purple Heart on D-Day. He has a good job in Modesto, and a girlfriend, and they are expecting their first child. Arresting Archie would be a tragedy to all those involved. Silas is the killer, manipulator, and thief. It's not Archie's fault.'

Red said, 'The law is the law. Archie was present during two of those murders.'

'Silas would have killed Archie, like he killed that poor kid up at the cabin, if he didn't help,' Reinhard protested.

Archie finally spoke, 'Sheriff, my father said, before I went in the army, he wouldn't hang anyone else until I returned. So, I stayed away. I didn't come back. Then I read that newspaper article. I don't know what made him start again, but you're right, I was there, I never should have kept my mouth shut, I'm as guilty as my father.'

Jim added. 'Well, Archie, I'd say both assessments by Red and Reinhard are correct. I will talk with the District Attorney and the District Court Judge to see where we go from here.'

Silas had been booked for the Hanging Murders and his arraignment would take place the following day.

Jim went over to the courthouse, next to the sheriff's department and down to the basement, where the jail was located. The cell containing Silas Reid was 6 x 9 feet, with one bed along the left wall. A sink and a toilet took up the opposite a corner. He put his arms through the bars and put his hands together. 'Silas, I need to ask a few questions. Was Archie an active participant in any Hanging Murders?'

'Shit, no! Sheriff, that weak, sniveling, mamma's boy couldn't piss and chew gum at the same time. I took him with me, but he was useless. He was worse when we went out hunting for deer or elk. A whiney cry-baby, afraid of the dark. When he didn't come back from the war, I was happy. Thought the Krauts had killed him. Minerva received a card late in '45 saying he returned but she didn't know if he was coming back to California.'

'Why did you start killing again?'

Silas snorted. 'I thought Woody would take over the family business, killing and robbing. Harris said he was setting up more robberies.'

'Did Harris know you were hanging people?'

'Hell no!' Silas looked off from the sheriff and thought about something, 'I don't think Barton knew, either. He may have guessed, but he never asked. The only thing we shared was Lottie.'

'Who killed Barton?' 'No idea. I told you that.'

'You did it. And I'm going to prove it.' Jim left Silas in his cell, knowing Silas was a sadistic psychopath without a conscience. Death in the apple green room at San Quentin was the only answer for someone like Silas Reid.

No matter what Jim thought, one question remained for the sheriff's department: Who killed Barton Haskel?

CHAPTER 79

Three days had passed since the capture of Silas Reid.

Red and his cousin. Theo Culpepper, the FBI Special Agent assigned to the Hanging Murder case, were in my office, along with Merrill.

'I've spent some time with Silas in his cell, and we've been talking about his life,' said Red.

'Pray tell,' Merrill asked, sarcastically, 'what did the murdering bastard say?'

'Our discussions included the nickname Sailor, given to Silas by his mother back in Oklahoma.' Red smiled a bit. 'It seems the little boy wanted a model of a navy ship for a present when he was around five or six. He would get dressed up as his sailor suit and chase all the other kids around the neighborhood. His mother called him Sailor one day and it stuck for the rest of his life.'

I interrupted Red. 'Minerva and Lottie must have known about the nickname when we interviewed them.'

'Of course, they did.' Nodding, Red continued, 'Silas said they called him Sailor around the house all the time. He even told me about why he started killing men back in Oklahoma, starting with his daddy.'

'I'm always curious,' said Culpepper, 'about what killers say started them off doing all the horrific things they do. What was Silas's reason?'

'Oh, it seems his drunken daddy wanted the moonshine Silas was cooking, along with all the profits he made from his work. His father told the boy the whiskey was made on his land, it belonged to him.'

'Greed,' Merrill said. We all chuckled.

'I can understand a son not wanting to give all business profits to his father,' I said. 'Silas say anything else of value?'

'He insisted he never meant to kill his daddy. He chalked it all up to an accident. Said he lost his temper. He dumped the body down a dry well and tried to forget.'

Merrill, Culpepper, and I all looked at Red with our mouths open, waiting for the next shoe to drop. He wasn't about to disappoint us.

'Silas claims he didn't think about the body in the well until two sheriff's deputies came around looking for his daddy. It seemed that his relatives were wondering where the father ran off to. He took the deputies out to the well and shot them both dead, then dumped the bodies down the well, too. He went back to the house, gathered up Minerva and little Archie and hightailed it out here, to Inyo County.'

Culpepper asked, 'Shit, Red. What happened next?'

'Well, I called up the local police in Oklahoma, where Silas and his family had been living.' Red stopped to drink some water. 'They rang me back this morning, they found bones in the abandoned well. Forensics will tell who they belonged to. The authorities want Silas to stand trial for those murders.'

'I sure don't blame the State of Oklahoma for wanting him brought to trial for killing two deputies. The state doesn't want anyone to think they can get away with that kind of thing,' Culpepper said. 'Not that killing innocent people is any less important.'

I knew what he meant. My thoughts went to the fact that Inyo County was safe from the Hanging Murderer at last.

'Who killed Barton Haskel?' I asked.

No one gave me even a guess answer to my question. Red asked, 'Where is Darren Harris?'

Everyone in that room would have bet their bottom dollar that this was Barton's murderer. All the reasons fell into place—motive, means, opportunity. Barton never would have expected what was coming.

'Thinking of everything and everyone involved in these two cases, and that Gates, Lottie, Minerva, and Harris all lied,' I said, 'did Lottie or Minerva have anything new to say, before they were released?'

'No, Jim, they didn't. But they know a lot more than they're letting on.' Red smiled. 'We'll have to see what they do to each other on their own. Let's see how long it takes for them to turn on each other.'

CHAPTER 80

Merrill was alone at his ranch house, drinking rye straight from the bottle. He missed being sheriff. The big man had another shot and realized that a life with Marlene was never going to happen. He knew he needed to find someone to spend the sunset years of his life.

Merrill decided on taking a trip to Mexico. A warmer place to find a companion for the rest of his days. He had heard stories of other men who went down there and never returned because the women knew how to treat a man right.

It didn't occur to Merrill that he needed to learn how to treat a woman right. He never looked back, never re-examined his past deeds, never apologized, and never accepted blame. The retired sheriff was an anachronism of a time when men ruled everything in life. Times were changing; how long this social attitude would last was unknown.

CHAPTER 81

Silas refused to implicate his son as an accomplice in the Hanging Murders in '40 and '42. Whether he did it out of disgust for his lie or whether he did it on purpose to save his son, I couldn't guess. The District Attorney and District County Judge concurred, Archie was free to go.

Archie said goodbye to his mother, he would see her soon, and bring Gretchen with him, and he and Reinhard were in Archie's 1947 Pontiac, headed back to the Central Valley and the sleepy town of Modesto.

Taking a deep breath, Archie said, 'I'm relieved now with Silas behind bars. Woody's murder was a tragedy I'm going to live with for the rest of my life. If only I went to find Silas sooner, Woody might still be alive now.'

'I know,' Reinhard said, 'but you can't live your life tormented by ifs onlys.'

Archie told Reinhard about the discussion he'd had with Minerva before leaving the family's ranch house. 'My mother admitted to me she allowed Silas to kill, and go on killing, all those years, just to save her own life. She hated Silas but allowed him to do whatever he wanted to save my life.'

Reinhard looked at his friend with a question on his lips.

Anticipating the question, Archie said, 'I'll tell my mom about her future grandchild when I bring Gretchen to meet her.' The two war buddies stopped and ate at a little Mexican restaurant in Bakersfield. The food was hot and the Cerveza cold.

As they went back to the car, Archie asked. 'When do you need to return to Chicago?'

'When you don't need me anymore. I called home and said I would return when you were back in Modesto with Gretchen. You know, a family run business can make allowances for a family member's absence.'

'If that is the case, buddy, then when we get to Modesto, you'll meet Gretchen, and see the sights.'

Laughing, Reinhard said, 'I can't wait for the opportunity to see the Central Valley.'

The men drove on, through the southern area of the valley. They stopped talking and were enjoying the cool evening breeze coming in through the car windows. The onion fields, which grew in the fertile acreage past Bakersfield, gave off their sweet aroma for miles as they drove north.

The music from the radio played familiar Big Band tunes of Tommy Dorsey, Benny Goodman, and Glenn Miller, and the men were reminded of their time in England before D-Day. Reinhard hummed along to the Glenn Miller Orchestra's snappy rendition of 'Chattanooga Choo-Choo,' performed by Paula Kelly and the Modernaires. Each was lost in his own thoughts about family, hometowns, girlfriends, and the future.

The song finished, and Archie slowed down, making a U-turn on California Route 99 and headed back the way they came. Archie had just realized something, as if a light had gone on in his head.

Reinhard was surprised by the sudden change in plans. He glanced quizzically at Archie. 'What are you doing?'

'We need to go back and talk to the sheriff.'

CHAPTER 82

Grady finished writing his latest article at the kitchen table in Edith's house and pulled out the last page from his portable machine. He was giddy with completing his piece. It was the final installment of his exposé concerning the Hanging Murders in Inyo County.

Edith came up beside him and leaned over his shoulder. She massaged his neck muscles as she read the text and put her arms around his neck, lightly kissing him, not wanting anything to change. In her mind, all was right with the world, and thoughts of settling down crept into her mind as never before. She relished sharing her house and her bed with Grady, star reporter.

Grady was fantasizing about his future. This series of articles would make his name. Moving on from the *LA Post*, and the notoriety of being a gossip columnist. Should he talk to the *LA Times*? Or go to another city, perhaps Chicago. Maybe Philadelphia? Or New York? Wherever he went in search of a new job opportunity, there was no room for Edith.

On a scale of one to ten, Grady rated Edith a marginal seven, good-looking, kind, generous, but too clingy, too opinionated. Grady was the man, he thought he should always make the decisions, set the rules, be in charge.

Now, he needed to drink a stiff double Scotch, remove his shoes and lift his tired feet off the floor. Edith wanted more of him now; the article finished, and her persistence was wearing him down. He turned to her, pulled her onto his lap with his arms tightly around her middle. They covered one another's mouth and drank the air out of each other's lungs. The heat was rising to a fever pitch when suddenly Edith stopped, pushing Grady's roving hand away.

'I just realized what your story doesn't answer,' she said. 'Who murdered Barton Haskel?'

CHAPTER 83

Conchita was unsure about returning to the ranch house, where she had worked and lived.

I'd made my home at Rosita's house, which they were all very gracious about. I didn't care where we lived, as long as we were together. The last time I was this happy was before I joined the army.

Reflecting back, I realize the time with Harriet was like a nightmare or time that never was. If I didn't have the last picture of Kendall, Harriet, and myself still at my parents' house, I don't think I would remember what the mother of my child looked like.

I couldn't recall talking with Harriet about work or life. Everything during my marriage felt contrived or forced. We never talked comfortably, joked, or enjoyed a sunset together. I came to think that the thirteen years we were married were never real. Now, I couldn't remember anything we did, or even dreamed about. The time together had coalesced into a black hole without an end. Time to let it go.

A week into my stay, Conchita and I ate dinner with her family, then Rosita, as always, made the children clean up the dishes.

We went to the bedroom together, earlier than usual. Conchita closed the door and leaned against it with her back. I put my arms around her waist. She put her hand on my chest, holding firm against me coming closer.

'We need to talk, Jim,' she started. 'Not about us, about murder, but not in front of the kids. That's all that's on your mind. Not you and me. Let's go through it find out what's keeping you up all night.'

Conchita was right. She was too smart for me. I wasn't sleeping well, and falling asleep was difficult most nights, even after we'd made love.'

'You're right, Conchita.' I took her hand and we sat on the edge of the bed. 'The Hanging Murders started in 1932, a short time after Silas came to California.' I thought it through. 'He murdered unknown men in '32, '34, '37, '40, and '42.'

Looking at her, I continued, 'Silas stopped because Archie went into the army. He promised Archie he'd wait until he returned. Archie didn't come home, and until Minerva received a birthday card, no one knew if he was alive or dead.' Grimacing with frustration, I went on. 'What forced him to wait fifteen years, even though Silas knew Archie wasn't coming home? You know, Silas did say one thing in jail, that Woody was being groomed to take over the business, but Woody needed to grow up.'

Conchita sat on the bed and looked at me. 'Jim, we already have all those answers. That's not what's tormenting you. You're avoiding the big elephant.'

She was right. And all day, no matter where I was, what I was doing, Barton's murder was rattling around in my head. 'The nightmares are about Barton's murder at Movie Flats. I never saw the car but I keep seeing it in my dreams.'

'Barton was shot in his head using his right hand, which you said he never used when shooting, right?'

'Right.'

'A note scrawled was placed on the passenger seat, all neat and tidy, right? So who wrote that note? Can you make everyone give handwriting samples?'

'Let's go.' I rose from the bed, took Conchita's hand, and we left the house. We headed for the sheriff's office.

CHAPTER 84

We arrived at my office in a rush. Brenda, the graveyard dispatcher, looked up from her desk with a big 'O' forming with her mouth. No one at the station knew about Conchita and me. We went into my office still holding hands. Our actions were sure to generate some reaction, once Marlene arrived for work at seven a.m.

Conchita sat in my chair behind the desk. I started thinking out loud.

'Who wanted him dead?' I began pacing around my office. 'Silas swears it wasn't him. Or Darren Harris. It could be either of them. Maybe Barton was sick of being on the other side of the law, maybe he was ready to turn himself in. John Gates was in Banning at the time of the murder. But we need to confirm that with eyewitnesses.' I stopped pacing.

Conchita asked, 'Would Woody want to kill Barton?' 'Barton? I can't see why? Silas, yes. How terrible his uncle

beat him to it.'

'Who saw Barton last?' Conchita asked, getting me back on track.

'Everyone at the bar, that Friday night.'

'Who did the abduction and where was he kept until the murder?'

'He could have been taken anytime early Saturday morning,' I said. 'From the autopsy, it doesn't look like there was a struggle.'

Before we could make any educated guesses, Grady and Edith came through the door to my office, all in a tizzy with the same question. 'Who killed Barton Haskel?' they asked in unison.

Shaking my head, I replied, 'That's what Conchita and I are just discussing. Who do you think?' Conchita and I faced Edith and Grady, we all looked at each other, not wanting to be the first to speak.

Breaking the silence, I said, 'Okay, let's all go to the conference room.'

We all filed into the room. Conchita, Edith, and Grady sat as I stood at the chalk board, writing. 'First, let's put down Barton, killed and left in the Movie Flats. Killed by a bullet to his right temple from his own revolver.'

I stopped, not wanting to give too much information, held back by my department, to Grady.

Grady said, 'Silas, the Hanging Murderer, is in jail and he was a partner with Barton and Darren Harris in the robberies.'

'He categorically denies killing Barton,' I said. 'Do you believe that?' Grady asked.

I shrugged.

Edith said, 'John Gates was in Banning when Barton was kidnapped and later killed.'

I shook my head. 'Edith, we think Gates was in Banning at the time, but don't know for sure. I will keep him on my list as the possible killer.'

'Barton would go with him willingly,' Grady said. 'He was his half-brother, right?'

So that information had gotten out?

Writing, I said, 'The two cowboys, Oakley and Mason, from the Circle W Ranch had a fight with Barton the night he went missing. Both were cleared by the ranch ramrod.'

Edith asked, 'What about Archie Reid? Isn't it a little odd that he just showed up now? After all these years? And with a buddy who looks like he could handle Barton with one hand tied behind his back.'

We all I heard the intercom click.

'Sheriff,?' It was Marlene's voice. So it was already after 7 a.m. 'I have Archie Reid on the phone.'

'I have it,' I said, and picked up the phone. 'Archie, what's going on?'

'Sheriff, Reinhard and I were driving up to Modesto, and I started to think, who killed Barton Haskel? I turned around and we're heading back. We've been driving all night.'

'Where are you now?'

'At a gas station on Highway 99. We're coming to the sheriff's office. We should be there soon.'

'Don't come here, go to your mother's house. Red and I will meet you there.' I looked at everyone. 'They're on their way back.'

'So, does Archie know who killed Barton?' Grady asked. 'We'll find out,' I said, but I didn't think so. He'd been away

too long.

Conchita asked, 'Barton had a relationship with Lottie, could she have lured Barton to come by the Reid house?'

'I don't think so, Conchita,' Edith said. 'I think Barton only slept with Lottie at his house.'

I didn't want to say it, but I was forced to. 'Barton was drugged with choral hydrate.'

Edith and Grady's mouths fell open with astonishment. The silence in the room was so quiet you could hear a pin drop.

Grady said, 'Whoa, pardner, what did you just say?'

'The official autopsy report states that Barton was given choral hydrate, a sedative, before he was shot.'

Grady said, 'Sheriff, I'm going to use this in my next article.'

'I understand, Grady, I expect you to, now that the case is almost over.'

'Almost over? We don't know who killed Barton, or why,' Edith protested.

I said, 'I know Edith, but for now we can only look at who is still alive, Minerva, Lottie, John Gates, and lest we forget, Darren Harris.'

Grady chimed in, 'Yes, the absconded Darren Harris, movie producer, bar owner, robber, and possible killer. Where is he, Sheriff?'

'I wish I knew, Grady. The word from the LAPD is he never returned to his house or the studio. Maybe he left the country.'

Conchita yawned and her eyes were drooping. I smiled at her, took her hand and pulled her up beside me at the chalkboard.

'That's it?' Grady asked. I knew he was anxious to get to his typewriter.

I was not about to give up my last ace in the hole, that Barton being left-handed. I couldn't give everything to Grady. 'There isn't anything else to say. I think you should all go home and get some sleep. I'll see what Archie has to say that's so important.'

Understanding they were not going to be part of this meeting, Edith and Grady reluctantly left the building.

'C'mon, Red and I will drive you home.'

I took Conchita's hand as we went out the front door together to the patrol car. As I opened the passenger's door, Conchita whispered in my ear how proud she was of me.

CHAPTER 85

Red and I, along with Rimmer and Roth in another patrol car, drove out to the ranch house of Silas and Minerva Reid. Archie and Reinhard, who had driven through most of the night, were not there yet.

When we arrived at the house, all was quiet. There was just a slight wind blowing from the west, dust and sagebrush blew past the front entrance.

I knocked on the front door. No answer.

A car was coming. It had to be Archie and his friend. Perfect timing.

Archie knocked, calling out, 'Mama, open the door.' Still no reply.

Archie turned the handle and opened the door and started to go into the house. I put out my arm and stopped him. 'Wait here. You, too, Reinhard.'

Red and I went into the house.

The silence was ominous, no sound, until a slight low moan came from somewhere.

Guns drawn, we made our way toward the sound, the living room. Minerva was sitting in the wingback chair, a little slumped to one side, holding a revolver in her right hand, dead from a single gunshot wound to her right temple.

Archie, right behind us, cried out, 'No! Mama, don't die! I am going to be a father. I want you to see your grandchild.' He wanted to pick up his mother and hold her next to his heart.

'Don't touch a thing!' I yelled out.

She looked at peace, rigor mortis was setting in. Her death had probably taken place between three and six hours before.

We heard the moan again, it was coming from behind the couch. Red pushed aside the furniture and discovered Lottie lying next to the wall, curled up in the fetal position. She held her abdomen as blood oozed from around her hands. Her hands were over a bleeding wound.

I shouted to the deputies outside, 'Get an ambulance out here! Lottie Pilgrim's been shot!'

Red held her head in his hands. Her moaning was low and guttural. Pushing aside the hair covering her face, he told her she shouldn't talk, the ambulance would soon get there, and that she needed to be strong.

'Minerva killed Barton,' Lottie said faintly. 'She shot me and then killed herself.'

With that, she seemed to drift into an unconsciousness state.

I stood and looked at Archie, who had fallen to his knees next to his mother, sobbing.

'Don't touch her,' I told him again.

Perry Rimmer was finishing a call. 'Sheriff, I called in for the lab people and mortician. It shouldn't take them long.'

The wail of the ambulance could be heard making its way up the road. I needed for them to save Lottie Pilgrim's life. And get the final word from the medical examiner after the autopsy of Minerva Reid.

CHAPTER 86

R ed's cousin, FBI Special Agent Theo Culpepper, who had assisted on the Hanging Murders investigation, came into the sheriff's office looking for Jim. It was now seven days since Silas's capture and two days since finding Silas's wife, Minerva, dead at her home.

Red came out from the back area and greeted his cousin. 'Morning, Theo, can I get you coffee?'

'Sure thing, Red, milk and two sugars.'

Theo sat sipping his steaming coffee. 'Congratulations on solving the Hanging Murderer case. After all these years. That's the good news. The bad news is, I came by to discuss some murders that have been occurring in other counties throughout Southern California. We seem to have a serial killer on our hands who has been flying under the radar for years.'

Jim could hardly believe his ears. All he could think was, Please not in Inyo County. We've had enough.

Theo continued, 'The only clue the police have in some of the jurisdictions is that an old faded blue or maybe black Chevy pickup truck, possibly a 40s' model, was seen in some of the locations of the murders. The FBI thinks it might belong to Silas Reid.'

Red shook his head. 'Silas doesn't own a Chevy pickup. Never did. Right now, his home is in the jail next door, awaiting trial.'

'What's the MO?' Jim asked, dreaded the answer.

'Stabbed. Stomach or heart. Tossed by the side of the road. No effort to hide the bodies. Mostly women, mostly young, but not all.'

'Never been one in Inyo,' Jim said. Silently, he added, thank God.

Red and Theo set down their coffee cups and went to the jail, next door in the courthouse, to Silas's cell for a little talk. What they found stunned them. Silas had hung himself, making a makeshift rope from his bed sheet and tying it above the highest crossbar of his cell. That was on Jim's watch.

'Well, doesn't that beat all hell?' said Red. 'The Hanging Murderer has saved the county from having to pay for a big trial. Yesterday, the fucking coward told us about the other murders he committed between 1932 and last year, all men in Southern California or just over the border in Nevada. No wonder he was willing to talk, he was bragging.'

Theo looked exasperated, now that he couldn't grill Silas about any of the murders in other counties.

'There is still someone you will be interested in talking to,' Red told his cousin. 'Minerva's sister Lottie, Silas's sister-in-law. She lived with Silas and Minerva for many years. She went through surgery successfully yesterday. She hasn't been cleared to talk to us, so Jim hasn't sat down with her yet but

CHAPTER 87

The day after Silas Reid hung himself, we received Minerva's autopsy report from Dr. Crawley at the Los Angeles Medical Examiner's Office. The report gave a unique narrative. I had been right, Minerva's death occurred three to six hours before we discovered her. A single gunshot to the right temple with a star shaped stippling around the wound, indicating the gun was held next to the skin. A single .22 round was found in the brain, matching the 22-revolver found in the deceased's right hand.

The supplemental findings were: 1. Stage four lung cancer, with metastatic finding in her bone and brain, 2. Chloral hydrate found in the stomach contents.

Red and I went to see Lottie in the hospital. She was awake and sitting up in her bed. It was now two days after we'd found her at the Reid house.

I started, 'Lottie, we have a few questions to ask about what happened with yourself and Minerva.'

Before I could say anything else, Lottie, blurted out, 'Minerva confided in me, she killed Barton Haskel all by herself. She wanted Silas arrested for the murder and out of her life for all the pain and suffering he put her and me and Archie through. After he killed Woody, she decided to make a clean breast of everything, wrote a note about her involvement and she called me into the living room. She shot me so her family could rest in peace together.'

Calmly I told her, 'Lottie, we never found a note on or near Minerva. We never found a note anywhere in the house. How do you explain that?'

'Sheriff, I saw the note before she shot me, I'm not making this up.' Lottie started to cry. 'My own sister shot me, she tried to kill me, Sheriff, for a crime she thought up and carried out.'

'Your gunshot wound was fresh, and Minerva had been dead for three to six hours before we arrived. What do you have to say about that?' Red asked

Lottie shrugged. 'I don't know medical stuff. I guess my hand must have kept the bullet hole closed.'

The silence in the room was deafening. Red and I waited for Lottie to say more. She stared into the distance, with a faraway look on her face, still whimpering through tears, not saying a word.

I asked, 'Lottie, how did you and Minerva get Barton to the house and overpower him?'

Lottie turned white, trying to hide her shock, hearing me say this.

'You called Barton and asked him to come to the house, didn't you? I bet you told him Silas was on his way and wanted to meet here, right?'

Lottie shook her head.

'Barton always met Silas here at your ranch house or the cabin in the mountains, never at his house in town, right?' Red asked.

Lottie was tearing up. 'I don't know, all I know is Barton came out to the house to wait for Silas and the next thing I know, he's passed out on the floor.'

'Maybe you and Minerva gave him some tea? He passed out a little while later, didn't he?'

Lottie didn't answer. She just rolled over on the bed into a fetal position and looked out the window, without saying another word. I could see she had a wry smile on her face as Red and I looked at each other. Before going to see her, we had decided to not mention the chloral hydrate.

I had one last card to play. 'Lottie, did you know Minerva had inoperable lung cancer?'

Lottie sat up suddenly. 'What? Sheriff, my sister was never sick a day in her life. She didn't have any cancer, don't soil my sister's name now that she's in Heaven.'

She turned back to face the window.

We left the room, letting Lottie believe that we bought her story.

Red was scowling as he shook his head. I knew he was angry.

'That woman lied to us, Jim.' Exhaling loudly, he continued, 'To think I once wanted to ask her out, I never in a million years would have suspected...' His rant petered out, without his finishing the sentence. I understood his frustration.

As I drove us back to the office, Red looked out the window, while I went over in my mind everything that had taken place since I returned to work.

We got to the station and went into my office.

I sat down and looked at Red. 'The wound to Lottie's abdomen made a decent size hole, but it was not life threatening. It went through her side and didn't hit any vital organs, even though there was a good amount of blood, Lottie's wound was too fresh to have happened when Minerva was killed. I think Lottie murdered Minerva and gut shot herself to make it look like she was the innocent party.'

Red was nodding his head in agreement.

'Proving my theory about Lottie as the killer of Minerva, as well as Barton, with the help of Minerva and possibly Woody will not be easy, since everyone but Lottie is dead.' I took out the autopsy report. 'We have time of death, drugging the victim, and lung cancer. With the information we have at present, proving in a court of law that Lottie killed Minerva would be difficult, but not impossible.'

'A good defense lawyer could say Lottie was shot at the same time as Minerva, difficult to prove differently,' Red noted.

'True. I think Lottie killed Minerva, but I want her for killing Barton. It would be hard to get a jury to convict Lottie for killing her sister, but getting them to convict her for killing Barton would be impossible, with the evidence we have now.'

Why am I holding back from charging Lottie? Is it because she took care of Kendall? Am I trying to save her because all the abuse she endured from Silas?

'If she killed Barton,' Red said. 'I don't think she did, Jim. I think it was Darren Harris. He had the motive.'

'What about the chloral hydrate?' I asked.

'Harris could have gone to see them, talk about Barton's death, slipped it into the tea.'

'Just Minerva's?' I asked. I kept thinking, what could the department do next? 'Red, we should let Lottie loose, for now. See what she does. We can charge her for Minerva any time.'

'We would need to keep a close eye on her,' Red said.

I was sure she and Minerva had dirty hands when it came to Barton Haskel's murder. The question was: who helped them manhandle Barton? Should I place my money on Woody? Or John Gates? Or was Red right, it was Harris?

'Red, call the Banning sheriff's office to ask them to keep an eye on John Gates,' I said. 'Besides Archie Reid, he's the only other relative from our cast of characters who's still alive.' Edith came in with a message from a doctor in Lancaster.

'Minerva Reid went to his office in September, he took X-rays, and then sent her to a Dr. Shapiro in Glendale. Dr. Shapiro is a surgical oncologist, a cancer doctor.'

I had to smile, Edith thinking I might know not know what a surgical oncologist does. I asked her, 'Did he mention if anyone was with Minerva?'

Edith replied, 'I didn't ask. I'll call the doctor.'

Soon, she came back into my office with the answer. 'Yes, her sister Lottie was with her.

CHAPTER 88

A month after Silas killed himself and took all the other information about his killings to the grave, Red received a phone call from his cousin, FBI Special Agent Theo Culpepper. 'Good morning, Red,' Theo opened. 'I'm calling to give you a follow-up on Silas Reid. I called Archie Reid in Modesto. He was hard to reach because he has taken on many

hours of overtime since he returned from Lone Pine.' 'And what did he say?' Red asked.

'He told me that he never went on any trips with Silas out of town. To his knowledge, Silas never owned or drove a Chevy pickup.' Theo paused a moment. 'Archie didn't like to hang around his father because Silas was a mean drunk, throwing things, yelling, cursing, and being a first-class asshole around Minerva. The kid said both mother and son stayed away from Silas as much as possible. The man never talked to them about his trips, he was always tight-lipped.'

'That's the same information we got,' Red said. 'Since Silas hung himself, have you heard of any new murders by the guy driving an old Chevy pickup truck?'

'No news from the FBI,' said Theo. 'It seems that our mystery murderer has taken some time off from his killing spree, but an update from the CHP. Seems he's a white guy, brownish hair, roughly forty-five years old and has an unkempt, shaggy beard.'

'Before I forget, Jim wants me to thank you and the FBI for your help putting surveillance in The Red Caboose in Banning. The Riverside Sheriff's Department has an undercover man keeping tabs on John Gates,' Red said. He and Theo and the sheriff of Riverside County had all worked together back before the war. 'Gates is Haskel's older half-brother. Different fathers.'

'Good idea,' Theo agreed.

'We know Gates is running The Red Caboose Bar & Grill for the elusive Darren Harris. No information on Harris yet, but it's a good bet he'll turn up there sooner or later. Oh…' Red tried to stifle a laugh '… Gates has a new lady friend, Sarah Palmer, aka Lottie Pilgrim.'

'No kidding. When did Pilgrim leave Lone Pine?' Theo asked.

'She moved out of the Reid's property, maybe three days after her discharge from the hospital,' Red replied. 'The place is abandoned now.

Theo said, 'Banning, yes, a lovely place if you like the heat at seven a.m. crawling up your body to unbearable in the afternoon to down-right unlivable by dinner time.'

'Banning is a hot, all the time,' Red said, 'and we're hoping it's a little too hot for Lottie.'

'Hey,' Theo said, 'maybe I'll head on down to The Red Caboose Bar & Grill in Banning. Have a beer, look for a Chevy truck, and ask Sarah Palmer out. See if she's a chatty date.'

Both men were laughing as they hung up.

The undercover man, Will Harper, was in place at The Red Caboose Bar & Grill in Banning. Harper, a sergeant in the Riverside Sheriff's Office, knew Culpepper and Fowler from different statewide sheriff conferences. He was to watch John Gates and Lottie Pilgrim, who was now Sarah Palmer, in charge of the books at the restaurant.

Harper, a twenty-five-year veteran in the Riverside Sheriff's Department, was a rail thin Black man who looked twenty years younger than his actual age of sixty. His sinewy, muscular six-foot frame made him look like a professional athlete instead of a lawman ready for retirement. He was the perfect person for the job. No one, not even the man who hired him, would suspect Will of being anything other than the worker he presented—the barkeep.

Will had been assigned to watch Lottie and Gates, like a fly on the wall, hoping to overhear anything which would incriminate either of them in the killing of Barton Haskell or Minerva Reid. Now, who would fall into the trap? Gates? Lottie? Darren Harris?

CHAPTER 89

The end of February came along, and crime was quiet in Inyo County. The temperature was warming up, and I was the happiest man in town. In Rosita's house, I found Conchita in the kitchen, pouring herself a cup of coffee. She turned toward me, and I placed my arms around her expanding waist and kissed her softly.

I let her go. I never knew what love was until I found Conchita. She taught me the meaning of love, to care for someone with all one's heart, unconditionally, no questions asked. To stand up for and behind the one person who means everything in your life. Now, hearing the news about our coming new addition, a child will make our life together that much more meaningful.

'I received a letter from Merrill today, over at the ranch.

He's decided to settle in Zihuatanejo.'

Conchita smiled. 'That's a sleepy little fishing village down by the Pacific Ocean. Only a few thousand people live there.'

'Sounds like it might suit his slower lifestyle,' I said. 'I hope he is finding his way down there. And guess what, he wants to give us the ranch as a wedding present.'

'That's very generous of him,' Conchita said, frowning, 'but I don't know if I want to live in that house again.'

'We can sell it and build another house on the land if you like,' I told her.

My life with Conchita felt right, more than right, better than at any time ever. I rested my chin on top of her head, looking out the window in the kitchen. I held her tighter, thinking about our baby coming in the fall. Whether it was a boy or girl was not a concern of either of us. We wanted a family together.

'I love you, Conchita, more and more each day. I want you to know, having you in my life completes me. I never imagined having my best friend, my wife, mother of our children, standing side by side with me, loving me more than I ever thought possible.'

'Jim, you saved my life. Without you, I don't what would become of me, I can't help loving you.'

CHAPTER 90

The March air was cool as Sarah entered the bar. She was returning from the California National Bank in the center of Banning with the daily deposit receipt for The Red Caboose Bar & Grill when she bumped into Will Harper, to her, the bar's sweeper. The time was eleven a.m.

Sarah apologized to the man who looked down on his luck.

Will and Sarah tried to walk past each other but kept moving in front of the other, not letting either move past the front door opening. 'I'm sorry, Miss Palmer, my mistake,' said Will as each party laughed in the bright morning sun.

The Riverside Sheriff's Department and the FBI had set up recording devices in the bedroom the two suspects shared, and every other room in the restaurant. A room in the building next door housed a deputy, listening in. The assignment, now three months running, was scheduled to last another month, unless something viable happened.

Harper hadn't noticed any slip-ups by Lottie, but he had noticed Gates getting close to the new waitress in the bar. If Lottie got wind of Gates two-timing her, Harper knew all hell could break loose.

'Will, have you seen John today?'

He mumbled. 'Where did I see Gates…? He's…uh…' The question seemed to fluster him.

Sarah had no time for this. 'Out with it. Where is he?' 'Come with me.' He led her to the back-storage room next

to the office and pointed to the shared wall between the two rooms. He directed her to put her ear next to the wall.

Will knew that every morning for the last week, Gates was having his way with the new waitress. He was hoping this would upset her so much she would turn on Gates and rat him out for the Haskel murder.

Sarah did as she was instructed and listened to the guttural sounds of two voices from inside the office. Her face went white. She left Will in the storage room, but she didn't go to the office from behind the bar, she retrieved the Remington Model 870 shotgun, 12-gauge, single barrel, pump with an 18-inch barrel. The weapon was fully loaded with five double-aught rounds, ammunition able to blow a person in half from ten yards away.

She racked a round into the empty chamber before she threw open the office door and watched John Gates work out his final hip thrusts.

Neither of the new lovers heard the door opening.

Sarah stood only eight feet away, raised the shotgun, rested the butt of the weapon next to her right hip for an easier reload without any kickback. Yes, Sarah Palmer, unlike Lottie Pilgrim, knew what exactly she was going to do.

Gates had his back to the door, away from his executioner.

Lottie screamed, 'You dirty, rotten, fucking bastard!' And then she fired her first round. The shot threw Gates sideways into the wall, nearly cutting the man in half, crumpling what was left of him on the floor.

Sarah pumped her shotgun again as the woman turned. Her mouth was open, unable to make a sound.

Will Harper, using his big right hand, took the shotgun from Lottie.

'Lottie Pilgrim, you're under arrest for the murder of John Gates.'

Lottie smiled. 'No, Will. My name is Sarah Palmer.'

'No ma'am, your real name is Lottie Pilgrim. Sarah Palmer is an alias you acquired when you left Lone Pine, and I'm Sergeant Harper, undercover with the Riverside Sheriff's office.

CHAPTER 91

Two days after the killing in Banning, Jim and Red were driving to the Banning jail.

'I just heard from Merrill, down in Mexico. You're not going to believe this, Red, but he ran into Darren Harris down in Zihuatanejo, of all places.'

'Mexico,' Red said. 'I called it, didn't I?

'It seems Darren, who now calls himself Doug Ellis, was telling stories about his exploits as a movie producer in Lone Pine. Merrill contacted the State DOJ. The local authorities locked up Darren and there are formal extradition proceedings to return him to California.'

Red smiled. 'Well, Jim, sounds like we have this case all wrapped up.'

'Not quite. We still need a confession. Lottie has to admit her part in Barton's murder. And hopefully implicate Harris.'

Jim parked in front of the jail. They sat in the patrol car for a few minutes, not saying anything else, each hesitant to come face to face with Lottie. Sighing, Jim opened his patrol car door.

'I'll put her in an interrogation room,' Deputy Stout said.

Lottie was wiped out from her latest ordeal. She sat in the chair, her lips cracked, dark circles under her eyes, and her hair in disarray, dirty and greasy from lack of care. Her eyes seemed clouded to Jim and her look reached to some far-off place he never saw.

'Lottie,' said Jim, 'this last action will send you to prison for the rest of your life. If not to the electric chair.'

She didn't answer or look at him.

Jim continued, 'Did you kill Barton Haskel?'

Lottie sighed and looked at the men. 'Minerva wanted to rid herself of Silas. John wanted Barton's job and position with Darren Harris. I wanted a better life. All my life, men took what they wanted from me, even my very dignity, and I didn't do a damn thing to stop them. Until now.'

There was silence in the interrogation room; Jim and Red waited.

'It started with my cousin, next door to our house in Oklahoma. It was kids having fun. I didn't know any better.' Lottie took a deep breath as she looked at them. 'I met Harlan when I was sixteen and we went out for a year. We finally made love in the back of his new Ford car. Woody came out of our tryst and Harlan was so happy he was marrying me. He told everyone how much he loved me, and I was the best thing ever in his life. I was the happiest girl in Oklahoma. In December of 1943, the War Department sent out two officers to tell me he'd died at the Battle of Tarawa. I was empty, lost, and had nowhere to go, me and Woody.'

She paused and frowned as she continued. 'Minerva wrote and said Woody and I should come out to Inyo County. It was God's country, clear blue skies, warm days, and friendly people. I wasn't in the house a week before Silas cornered me.

Minerva knew, she let it happen.'

Lottie looked at Jim Cobb with haunting eyes. 'Sheriff, women are stupid when it comes to men. Silas introduced me to Barton, I thought he was in love with me. I just did whatever they wanted to keep from getting hit, or worse, if I refused.'

She rubbed her lip. 'Barton met Lara Aartz. That's when John showed up. John Gates. He said all the sweet things I longed to hear. I fell again, like a dumb, lovesick cow. John opened the door to killing Barton and we could have everything. John told me that we would find happiness. All I had to do was kill Barton, I could do it because he trusted me. All we had to do was make it look like a suicide. I didn't do it for the money, I did it for all the pain Barton caused me. But killing doesn't create happiness. I came down to Banning to start a new life, with a new name, and a man who told me he loved me. What a joke!'

Shaking her head, she continued, 'I only wanted to be loved and to love someone in return, not allow myself to be abused and taken advantage of. Is that such a crime?'

'No it's not, Lottie,' Jim said, 'but killing three people is.'

Lottie stopped talking, and the interview was over as far she was concerned. She turned away from them, toward the wall.

'I have one more question. The coroner found traces of chloral hydrate in Minerva's stomach when he performed the autopsy. The same substance found in Barton Haskel's stomach. Lottie, where did you get the chloral hydrate?'

Lottie looked at the wall, silent, without acknowledging this last question.

Jim patiently waited for her to respond. She never did answer Jim's question.

Proving this wasn't necessary to put Lottie Pilgrim alone in a six-by-nine-foot jail cell for the rest of her life, or even possibly get the death penalty.

There wasn't anything else to ask of the broken woman as she physically aged in front of Jim and Red. One part of their souls reached out to the woman who had endured so much hardship, while their practical, law upholding side wanted to put the killer in jail and throw away the key.

Twelve jurors in the state of California would decide the fate of Lottie Pilgrim: Murder for John Gates, with a seat in the apple green room where potassium cyanide pellets were mixed with sulfuric acid, generating hydrogen cyanide gas, or life in prison.

CHAPTER 92

I started the patrol car with Red in the passenger side for the ride back to Independence.

'Jim, my hope is that the DA will talk with her lawyer, who will get her to plead guilty to all the murders in front of the judge and a trial won't be necessary.'

I replied, 'We can only hope. I don't want to go through a long, drawn-out trial. Reliving all the details of the case is definitely not what I look forward to. We have her cold for Gates. If her confession of the murder of Barton, and possibly Minerva's murder is included, good. Either way, our job is done.'

Red nodded his head. 'I want to have a nice quiet remainder of the spring and summer.'

Agreeing, I said, 'My friend, I want the same. I do have some news on a happier note. Conchita and I are expecting our first child this fall.'

Smiling, Red said, 'That's fantastic news, I'm so happy for you both. Soon we will have a little Cobb running around the station.'

We smiled, not paying attention to anyone or anything else in the world.

CHAPTER 93

The two lawmen from Inyo County drove straight out the main road along Route 60 from Banning. They didn't see the old Chevy truck, the one with the worn out dark blue color, pass them coming from Beaumont.

The man wondered if Banning was a good place for Mexican food and slowly passed The Red Caboose Bar & Grill.

THE END

ACKNOWLEDGEMENTS

Again, thanks to Audrey Lintner of ALTO Editing Services for all the work performed for this novel. I especially want to thank Jim Bilyeu again, a retired Deputy of the Inyo County Sheriff's Department. No book is all one person's work, it takes many people to get to the finish line, my heartfelt thanks to my manuscript editor—Yvonne Blackstone from Blackstone editing. I want to thank my literary agent—Jan Kardys for her belief in myself and my work, and the co-agent from Black Hawk Literary Agency—Barbara Ellis.